Infidelity . . .

Unconventional behavior certainly is not rare in Manhattan art circles. But what was going on in the menage of the Byrne woman raised the eyebrows even of the most broadminded. For she was supposed to be loving and cherishing another artist, Greta. Yet she welcomed the advances of bewitching young Paula Temple.

THREE WOMEN
by March Hastings

THREE WOMEN

by March Hastings

The Naiad Press, Inc.
1989

Printed in the United States of America
First Naiad Press Edition

Three Women *first appeared as a paperback original novel published by Universal Publishing and Distributing Corporation in 1958 at the beginning of the era referred to as the golden age of lesbian paperback originals.*

Cover design by Pat Tong and Bonnie Liss
    (Phoenix Graphics)
Typeset by Sandi Stancil

Library of Congress Cataloging-in-Publication Data

Hastings, March.
    Three women / by March Hastings.
        p.   cm.
    ISBN 0-941483-43-6 : $8.95
    I. Title
PR9619.3.H34
[T47 1989]   89-34016
823—dc20   CIP

Part One

1

He lurched at her from the doorway. Flakes of snow glistened on his straggled eyebrows. She smelled the stench of whiskey in his clothes.

"Go on, mister. Keep moving." Paula jostled him away with her free hand and hurried along First Avenue. The freezing streets were slippery beneath her boots but she plunged forward, splashing into lakes of snow and ice gathered at the curb. She hated these winter nights worse than the steaming nights of summer. The wind tore savagely at her face. It seeped in past the woolen scarf and settled bitterly around her neck beneath the chestnut hair. As far as she could see the Avenue was black and lonely. But she knew that men huddled in corners, some asleep and not feeling the cold, others alerted by wild visions more fantastic than the freezing, howling night around her.

With the container of milk hugged close, she hurried into the entrance of the tenement and through the narrow hall strewn with garbage the kids had pulled out of cans. She clomped up the three flights lighted by weak bulbs and let herself into the apartment. This wasn't home to her. It was the place where Ma and Pa and Mike and she happened to live because it was cheaper for everyone to live together there.

She set the package on the small table in the foyer and hung up her coat and scarf on the hook beside Mike's leather jacket.

"That you, Paula?" Her mother called from where she stood at the stove, moving a big wooden spoon in a pot of rice.

You could see the kitchen from the foyer. You could see the bedroom beyond the kitchen where Mike sat cross-legged, reading an airplane magazine like he was in his own private library on Fifth Avenue.

"I just made it," Paula said, breathing on the tips of her fingers to get out the sting. "He was just about closing when I got there." She brought in the paper bag and pulled out the container of milk.

Why did her Pa always have to get his attacks late at night? Why didn't he stop drinking so he could eat meals like a normal person? She wanted to respect him but it was hard not to get angry at a man who insisted on killing himself, eating away his

4

stomach with poison that didn't even give him pleasure anymore. She poured milk into a saucepan and set it on the stove beside the rice.

"I wish we could keep some extra around for times like this," Paula said. She didn't want to tell her mother about the nastiness with that man outside. When a girl gets to be eighteen, there's no excuse for being afraid. You comb your hair down long around your shoulders and wear the kind of clothes that show off your body so that men will look at you. And you just hope they're the right kind of men. If it happens to be the other kind, you fight your way through and hope for better next time. Because, she guessed, that's life.

Paula took a bowl from the cabinet on the wall and held it while her mother spooned in a mushy helping of rice, straining the starchy water out against the side of the dented pot. Then she spilled the warm milk on top and set the bowl on the checked oilcloth that covered the kitchen table.

"Your father's in the bedroom. Why don't you go see if he wants to eat?"

For the first time, Paula smiled. She knew her mother was thinking the same thing she was thinking. But Ma was the kind of woman who never told her husband what to do.

"Sure, Ma," she murmured with sudden softness. Her mother had black hair that she wore braided and coiled on the back of her head. It was the one really neat thing in the whole place and Paula liked to look at it sometimes. It made her feel ladylike and uncluttered and gentle to look at her mother's shining hair.

In the bedroom her father lay on his side, knees

pulled up almost to his chin. He bit his lip and squinted at the wall, mute with pain. Heavy flowered curtains at the window made the room seem smaller and warmer. The silver crucifix above the bed glowed with half-reflections from other rooms. Paula sat down beside her father and put a hand lightly on his arm.

"Pa," she said softly. "Pa, you want to come in and have something? You'll feel better." She didn't know why she should feel sorry for him. For that matter, Paula didn't know how she could hate and love him at the same time, but she did.

Pa didn't say anything. He looked at her and squeezed her hand. The sleeve of his long underwear had a ladder-like run in it. Pale skin showed through, strangely smooth like a baby's. Her own skin had that same delicate quality so she could never get really tan in the summer.

Maybe she loved him because she remembered how they used to play at Coney Island and those white arms would hold her safely above the huge and thundering waves that rolled in.

"Maybe, if I brought it in here," she continued, "you could take a few spoonfuls?"

"No." The voice was a grunt. "I'll come inside. In a minute." His body twisted suddenly in pain.

She waited for the spasm to pass then helped him sit up. Iron grey bristles on his chin made him look older than forty-five and he breathed heavily like a very old man, clinging to the edge of the bed with trembling hands.

Her arm around his waist, his weight full against her, Paula helped her father out of the room. They passed the dresser near the door, and she noticed for

6

the thousandth time her parents' wedding picture. It looked almost like new, the faces smiling and proud. For the thousandth time she thought: This will happen to me too. It happens to everybody.

In the other room Mike lit his new corn cob and sweet-smelling clouds followed Paula and her father into the kitchen.

She wanted to go to sleep because tomorrow was a big day. But she waited to clean up like she always waited. Phil would tell her she looked great anyway; she knew that. Besides, no matter how she felt, she never looked tired in the green dress.

It was past one o'clock when she finally wound the big alarm clock and crawled into bed. The knowledge that it wouldn't have to ring tomorrow gave her a sense of freedom and comfort. She snuggled under the rough wool blankets, adjusted herself around the lumps in the mattress, and thought of Phil, smiling, till she drifted into sleep.

Fiercely bright, the sun stabbed at Paula's eyes. She turned to escape back into darkness but it was too late. The heavy odor of coffee came to her nostrils and she heard her father snap on the radio to the nine a.m. news. Cups and dishes rattled in the kitchen where Mike was cramming breakfast because the gang was waiting for him in the clubhouse.

Struggling up from under the covers, she stared out to the cloudless sky alive with golden light. The windows faced the courtyard. As she grew slowly more awake, her ears caught the sound of kids yelling as they threw snowballs at each other. With a sigh she lifted herself on both elbows and tossed the tangled curls back from her shoulders.

Saturday. Good to be alive on Saturday. No rush hour, no switchboard. Lazy, wonderful Saturday spreading around you, letting you believe it was forever.

She slid out of bed, glad that she had forgotten to pull the shades down, and stood in the play of sunshine. She stretched in its warmth and smiled dreamily. The linoleum felt smooth and cool to her bare feet. She picked up her skirt and sweater and padded into the bathroom. The big water box gurgling above the toilet all the time didn't irritate her this morning. She splashed water on her face and neck to wash rather than waste gas to heat up enough water for a bath. Later she would take a long hot bath till her body glowed.

By the time she came in for breakfast, the meal was ready and Mom had the shopping list all made out. Paula ate a scrambled egg with two pieces of toast that had charcoal marks across them from the toaster coils. But even the burnt part tasted good to her this morning. Anything would.

Imagine: Phil wanted to show her off to the relatives! And to Aunt Bernadette, of all people. The aunt who paid for trade schooling and down payments on cars and — and marriages.

The thought of Aunt Bernadette propelled Paula happily through the supermarket crowds of people and baskets. She wheeled her own cart skillfully, tossing lunchmeat on top of jello on top of soapflakes. The fact that Mike was certainly old enough to help didn't occur to her as she hefted a heavy bag in either arm and pushed her way out.

8

Mom, in the same apron that she had been wearing all week, checked the list of prices against the items and dropped the pennies into an old preserve jar behind the salt shaker.

"I don't know," she said. "Maybe Mike should get a part time job."

"Fat chance," her father snorted and opened the paper that Paula had brought.

"When is that boy going to stop living in his own world?" her mother mumbled.

"When he gets a girl," Paula said. "A girl is what makes a man a man," she said wisely.

Her father laughed with affection. "Don't you know it," he said.

"Yes," Paula answered, trailing off to take the bath she had promised herself. As she closed the door to the bathroom, she heard her mother's voice. "You shouldn't joke that way with her. That child doesn't know as much as you think."

Oh, don't I know!

Paula grinned and released a spluttering stream of hot water into the tub. She knew sitting upstairs in the movies with Phil's leg pressed against hers. She knew her own softness pulled up tightly to the muscles of his body hard under the material of his shirt. She knew the thrilling strength of his lips seeking eagerly into the curve of her throat.

She knew a lot, thought Paula. Almost everything.

Gingerly she put a toe into the steaming water, then lowered herself slowly, wincing until her skin became accustomed to the heat. She stretched out and lay for a while, feeling her body trying to rise in the full tub of water, watching the small waves lap across her young bosom.

She wished she were big up top like some of the movie stars so that full flesh would swell over the neckline of her dress. If she had that kind of body, she would wear a small golden heart on a chain just long enough to point there and attract attention to what she had.

Suddenly a little embarrassed at herself, she grabbed the cake of soap and began lathering her body furiously.

Small curls clung damply to her forehead as she rubbed her arms and back vigorously with the towel a few minutes later. She sprinkled herself generously with lilac talc and discovered there wasn't enough left for between her toes. She hated to cover the gentle fragrance with bra and girdle but it gave her pleasure to slide the sheer stockings over her legs; the seams brought out the length and curve of what Phil called her "cheesecake gams." Oh, he was a dear sweet wonderful guy. And she couldn't imagine that even after twenty years he would take her for granted. Having Phil made her feel lucky, almost charmed.

She took the green dress out of the closet and brushed it carefully. Though it hung two inches away from all the other clothes jammed into the tiny space, a small wrinkle showed across the lap. Paula frowned at it and stretched the material taut, holding it like that for a minute, but the wrinkle was still there after she zipped herself into it, so she smoothed and smoothed hopefully. From a cardboard box she took out a strand of pearls and matching earrings. For Aunt Bernadette she thought she'd better be conservative. Besides, she looked her best when she dressed simply, more mature and well brought up somehow. She blotted the lipstick and smiled at herself to see if any of it had gotten on her teeth.

Giving her hair a last flick with the comb, she took a breath and waited for Phil's double knock at the door. She didn't expect him to be on time. He had always been five minutes late ever since they started dating nine months ago because he usually forgot his keys and had to go back up for them. They made a joke out of this key business. Ever since his folks separated, his ma had started locking the door when Phil went out. He just never got used to it.

Anyway, Paula was ready ten minutes early. She looked around the bedroom for something to do. She didn't want to go into the kitchen and risk getting messed up, so she picked up a pencil and started nervously to sketch a face on the back of an old envelope. All the envelopes and margins of newspapers and backs of bills had Paula's doodlings on them. Sometimes she copied a landscape from a calender, or a face. Back in high school, she had gotten the best marks in art class. Her pictures hung around the room during Open School week.

The double rap sounded lightly on the door and startled her. She dropped the pencil, grabbed her best coat and ran out to greet Phil.

"Well, hi." A grin danced over the rugged face and brought out a dimple near the side of his mouth.

"Hi, yourself," she answered, standing with the coat on her arm so he could admire how the dress fit and outlined her body.

He took the coat and held it for her. The top of her head just about reached his shoulders, the kind of broad shoulders that made all his jackets look padded.

11

She liked his bigness and the darkness of his skin. Phil was like a wall she felt she could stand behind whenever she was cold or afraid.

"Did you notice?" he said. "I'm on time." He tapped his trousers pocket. "Ma's got a new system. She puts the keys in my pants before I get dressed."

Paula noticed that he was wearing a new dark blue suit. The color made him look even darker, almost Arabian. If you didn't know Phil, she thought, he could look like the most mysterious person in the world.

He came inside and said hello to Paula's folks then said he couldn't sit down for a minute. They had to run.

Paula followed him out and clattered down the stairs after him. It was fun trying to keep up with him in her heels. The big steps he took equalled three of her own.

Out in the street he put an arm around her and led her to the old Ford that had been his father's. His coat lay across the front seat and he tossed it carelessly into the back.

He started the motor. Then he turned suddenly and grabbed her to him.

"No," she protested in a thin voice. "I want to stay neat."

"Oh, hell. What for?" His black eyes flashed smiling at her and the dimple danced. She smelled the briskness of his after-shave lotion and lightly kissed a razor nick on his chin.

"For your aunt, silly. Don't you want me to look perfect?"

"You always look perfect. She's not going to care what you look like anyhow."

"Women always notice what other women are wearing."

"That's what you think." He flicked the earring on her lobe, and then eased the car out into traffic.

Paula arranged herself more comfortably and took a pack of cigarettes from the glove compartment. "That's not what I think. It's what I know. Honestly, you men are so conceited. Do you all think women only look at you?"

"They're wasting their time if they don't," he chuckled. "Besides, Bryne's a regular guy. You'll see."

She let him win the argument; it was easier. Besides, it was better that way. She just wanted to sit and watch his big hands on the wheel. For all their size and strength, the fingers were trimly masculine so that she felt clean and beautiful when they touched her.

The afternoon traffic captured them on Lexington Avenue and she thought she should let Phil concentrate on the driving rather than talk to him. She lit a cigarette and put it between his lips. He let it droop from his mouth, squinting one eye against the rising smoke.

"You know," he said, "I really hope the old gal takes to my idea. Boy, would it be a big step in the right direction."

Paula caught the sudden seriousness in his voice and she realized that Phil was really depending on this afternoon. It never occurred to her that he would ever depend on anything except his own efforts.

"Well, of course she'll go for it." She filled her own voice with certainty. "It's a very sensible idea. I could see where she would hesitate if you wanted to start out in a new business of your own. But buying

13

a partnership in that paint store — that's a going thing, for sure. Nobody with any brains would turn down such an offer."

"I guess you're right." He pulled up for a red light and flicked the cigarette out of the window. "I guess you're pretty damned right all the time. Aren't you, honey?" He leaned over and kissed the tip of her nose.

The comfort of his compliment settled around her like the warmth of a blanket. She knew that Aunt Bernadette would give him the money. And then — then the world would open wide for Paula, too.

A poodle with a pink bow on its head looked at them from the car alongside and he pointed it out to her.

"You want to raise dogs someday? Lots and lots of puppies?"

She felt her face go warm and she couldn't think of some quick, smart response.

"Oh, my baby's blushing!" He laughed. "We'll take care of that later."

The car jumped forward again and she was glad that he had to keep his eyes on the traffic.

Aunt Bernadette lived in a brownstone house on East Eleventh Street. They drove slowly by, looking for a place to park. Slim trees ringed with metal guards lined the sidewalks and Paula thought how green and lovely it must be here in the springtime. This was the kind of street you can stroll along on a Sunday afternoon, quiet and pleasant and neighborly. On a street like this, you didn't yell after your

14

friends; you walked to reach them and then only chatted in a normal tone of voice.

Phil found an empty space near the corner and they had to walk halfway back. In her mind Paula prepared herself for sitting properly in an old fashioned chair and sipping tea from a delicate china cup. She hoped Aunt Bernadette would think she was a lady and a suitable companion for her nephew. If the old lady approved of her, she might be more kindly disposed to Phil's proposition. Yes, Paula could help Phil appear serious and capable.

They reached the flight of steps. For a second she took Phil's hand and squeezed it.

"Stop worrying," he said.

She smiled weakly and followed him up to the shining black door.

Aunt Bernadette's apartment was on the main landing. Paula patted her hair a last time as Phil lifted the brass knocker and let it drop.

They waited a few seconds before Paula saw the door knob turn.

"Hello," the woman said as she opened the door, and Paula wondered if Aunt Bernadette were sitting in the parlor somewhere.

Phil pushed her inside and at the same time kissed the woman a big smack on the cheek.

"Paula, this is my Aunt Byrne," he said.

For an instant Paula could do nothing but stare at the woman. This was Aunt Bernadette? she thought. Paula had expected wrinkles, but not a crease marred the face of this tall, stately, somehow ageless woman. The sun gleamed on her red blonde hair that fell in a soft wave to just below her ears. No pins held it in place and the hair tumbled at random like a young boy's. Her hazel eyes slanted upward, large, almond-shaped, with a sly smile darting behind them. The clear skin with a hint of freckles across the nose was the kind of skin you wanted to touch and caress with your hands.

Paula remembered herself with a start and said, "How do you do." Her voice almost cracked.

"Please call me Byrne," the woman replied in a casual tone.

Instinctively Paula knew this person understood her nervousness. Phil helped her off with her coat and threw it on the low modern chair that stood near the window.

The huge living room was sparsely but comfortably furnished with simple things that gave Paula the feeling of easy living, easily acquired.

As Byrne motioned her to a chair, she noted a heavy gold ring on the fourth finger of her right hand. It was an ornate ring, without stones, almost like a wedding band. The fingertips shone with colorless polish.

"Has it been two years, Phil?" she said. "Or more? I seem to have forgotten that my nephew is this much of a man." She stood beneath a large oil painting, with one arm leaning on a shelf of books. The white silk shirt fell in graceful folds down the long curve of her torso. Charcoal slacks picked up the line of her hips and carried the design of her body down to thonged sandals.

"Quit kidding," Phil laughed nervously. Paula could tell he was nervous because of the quick way he was breathing. He put his hands in his pockets and jangled the keys as he walked around the mosaic coffee table, sat down on the edge of a chair, got up

16

again. "We saw each other at Frankie's wedding last year. And I haven't changed at all since then. Except maybe something has been added, at that." He winked at Paula.

Paula nodded, wondering why Phil was acting like such a child before this sophisticated woman.

Byrne tilted her head and gazed steadily at Paula. "You added wisely," she replied. "I congratulate you."

Desperately Paula wanted a cigarette. Her palms were perspiring. She felt sweat coming off on the material of her purse, but if she moved her hands, a dark stain would be noticeable and Byrne would see how ill at ease she really was.

Paula wanted to say something complimentary in return. She couldn't just sit there forever, like an idiot.

"You have a lovely home," she managed. "I think that's a beautiful painting." She nodded toward the nude figure of a woman seated on a plush stool. The back of the woman faced out and the light illuminated the lines of her shoulders and the curve of her back till the eye came to rest on the fullness of her buttocks. Paula had never realized before that a woman could look good from the rear like that. This one was beautiful.

"Byrne painted that herself," Phil said.

"No. As a matter of fact, I didn't." She moved her hand up through the back of her hair and Paula caught the glint of fuzz on her neck. It made her shiver oddly. "I haven't lifted a brush for too long. That one is the gift of a student and friend."

"I'm sorry," Paula said before she could stop herself.

17

Byrne turned full around and examined her curiously. The reddish eyebrows were so even and regular and lay so flat that they looked darker. "Sorry? For heaven's sake, why, child?"

The word "child" made Paula's throat tighten but she went on, a little flustered. "Because people who do something that they enjoy can't be too happy when they stop." She clutched her purse and bravely held her glance directly on Byrne.

She saw the woman's lips part just the smallest bit as though she were about to question further. But evidently she thought better of it and the mouth spread into an appreciative smile.

Phil said, "Don't tangle with Paula. She was the champion drawer in senior class. She may even be a frustrated artist, for all I know."

"Do you paint, Paula?"

"No." She dropped her glance to the sandals, wishing she hadn't brought up the topic.

Byrne persisted, "Why not?"

"Oh, she's got better things to do," Phil put in.

"Why don't you paint?" Byrne seemed not to have heard him.

"Oh, I'm not that good." She tried to pass it off. "Doodling is more my speed, I guess."

"And I keep her pretty busy, you know. Paula is a serious type. She's not going to be one of those Bohemian mothers in dungarees and neglected kids."

Paula knew he was edging in to talk about the store and she hoped Byrne would let him get to the topic. She didn't know how to handle herself with this woman — Byrne paid attention to her as though she, Paula, were the important individual instead of Phil. She felt flattered by the woman's interest but

18

couldn't explain it to herself. Why should she care if I paint? Why does she look at me and not at my clothes? A weird feeling rose in her and brought with it vague longings always resting somewhere dark and unheard. If only she could run away before Byrne saw too deeply. But she knew it was too late and that really, she didn't want to run at all. She wanted to stay and let Byrne go somehow deeper, deeper until she could tell Paula what herself really was.

Phil lit his third cigarette and was motioning through the air with great display of self-confidence. "Paula isn't one of those hare-brained beauties you see every day. She's the kind who helps a man make his way in the world."

"I understand," Byrne said, patting Phil's shoulder to tell him without words that he could stop raving now. "What say we drink to making one's way in the world?" She found three highball glasses in a cabinet built into the wall and put them on the table. "Scotch? Bourbon?" She looked at Paula. And Paula knew that Byrne knew she didn't drink.

"Scotch'll be fine," Paula said.

Phil got ice and poured the drinks.

Paula sipped at hers and didn't like the bitter taste. Phil took long swallows, trying to fill himself with the strength to bring up his reason for being here.

Byrne saved him the trouble. She settled herself into the couch and crossed her legs. "Now tell me, little nephew, what can I do for you? I don't suppose you're here to socialize with your ancient relative."

Paula thought: Ancient? You'll be young forever.

"Well, the truth is," Phil eased his way slowly, "I could use a little help if you want to give it."

19

"Of course."

"There's this paint store on the corner of Third Avenue in the Seventies. Mueller's. Maybe you've heard of it. They advertise in the buses."

"I don't ride buses."

"Anyway, it's a real good thing, this store. Busy, large. And it's established. I have a chance to buy a partnership because one of the men is selling out and his son happens to be a friend of mine. If I could get in there . . ."

"What do you know about the business?"

"What's there to know?"

Paula hoped he would say something that sounded smart. She didn't like the way he was appealing to Byrne. As though she were the man and he a child — that's how he sounded.

"Assuming there isn't anything to know, how much do you need?"

He took a long breath. "Ten grand." Putting his tongue in his cheek and making it bulge, he watched to see how she would react.

"That's a lot of money for you, my boy."

"I'll be able to pay it back. You'll get a part of it every six months."

"That's not the point." She set the half empty glass on her knee. "I simply hope that you've chosen wisely. That size investment will make a responsible citizen of you overnight. Are you sure you want to sell paint for a living?"

"I can't be a crumby mechanic's helper all my life," he blurted. "This is the kind of opportunity that gives a man a chance to be something. Get himself away from those lousy tenements."

"And give him a chance to raise a decent family," Byrne added, glancing at Paula.

"Right!"

"Oh, I don't know," Byrne shrugged. "You might just as well do this as anything. It sounds reasonable enough to my unreasonable mind." She finished her drink and set it on the long table. "Sold, Philip. There's no reason why I should give you a hard time when all this money came to me so easily." The hint of some unrelenting memory shadowed her words.

Phil hadn't expected her to agree so quickly. He sat on the edge of his chair, his long-winded efforts to convince her further abruptly interrupted.

"But if I were you," she added more brightly, "I'd stock some art supplies for Paula. She may be wanting to experiment one of these days."

Phil found himself. He came out of the chair and filled Byrne's glass again. "Oh, you're a pal. You're a real pal." He couldn't find an expression big or grand enough. "I love you!"

Not knowing what to do, he bent over and kissed Paula. She moved back from his touch, self-conscious in the presence of this woman.

She wants me to paint, she thought. Without knowing whether I can do anything or not, she's interested in me.

Paula looked past Phil, intensely wanting Byrne to say something more.

Byrne smiled at her, more with her eyes than with her lips, and said, "You are going to try it, you know."

"I'd make a terrible pupil." Paula flushed. She realized that she had practically asked Byrne to teach her.

"Perhaps." Byrne's eyes slowly closed and opened again, changing the grey-green depths to clear emerald. "Perhaps not." Paula felt a tightening thrill at the somehow unnamed implication in Byrne's voice.

To be polite Phil talked on for another fifteen minutes, exuding energy and success, the dimple flitting in and out of his cheek. He stood taller, filling the room with his dark massive physique. He told Byrne pieces of family news. She listened, obviously without interest, nodding occasionally or making some brief comment that showed Paula just how little she really cared about her family. She wondered what this woman did care about. Not money, certainly; not ambition. Without knowing why, Paula wanted this strange person to care about something, anything, to care very much.

Finally, Phil picked up Paula's coat and helped her into it. She buttoned it slowly. Byrne walked with them to the door.

"I'm glad I met you," Paula said in a low voice.

"Are you?" Byrne closed one button she had missed and held her hand there for a moment.

Paula held her breath till the woman released her. She took Phil's arm and moved backward through the doorway.

In the cold darkness of Phil's Ford, Paula shook herself, realizing that every muscle in her legs ached intensely. She shook herself and tried to stretch out the knots.

"Oh, baby," Phil whispered. "This is it."

"I'm so happy for you." She let him lean across

to her and put his mouth on hers. Through the coat she felt the pressure of his hand against her breast.

"It's all right," he said. "It's good. I want to marry you. I'm going to love you forever and we'll have all the good things. No struggling like our folks, honey. Just lots and lots of loving."

He moved his head down and rested his cheek against her chest. She looked past him at the lights on the avenue.

"I'm asking you to be my wife," he whispered. His voice seemed to come to her from far away.

She put her lips into his hair and inhaled the sweet male smell of hair tonic. "Oh, yes," she murmured. "Oh, yes."

I'm going to be Mrs. Carson, she thought. I'm going to be the wife of this boy. But her feeling was not the fantastic delight she had always expected. With a touch of fright, she realized that this was like seeing a play by sixth graders after having been to Broadway.

She decided that she was tired; that her brain must be as numb as her body. Tomorrow she would know the full meaning of his words and her whole being would burst into the sky in overwhelming celebration.

They stayed quietly together in the darkness until she felt the cold beginning to creep back into her limbs. "Please start the car," she said, "and turn on the heater."

"You're so practical," he replied, sitting up and turning the key in the ignition. "Where's your romance? We've been going together so long, you must think we're married already."

"That's true," she agreed. Maybe that's what it

was, actually. She hoped so. With all her heart she hoped so.

"It's still early," he said. "We can go up to Jack's place. I told him not to be home tonight."

"You what?"

"That's right. I knew I was going to ask you tonight, Byrne or no Byrne. I love you so much, Paula. You know how much I love you. But I've never really touched you. Not all the way. And I can't stand it. Not tonight, I can't. Even with all the world so good to me, the one thing that will make it really important is having you. And since we're getting married . . ."

Wildly she thought: I'll go with him. I'll give him everything he wants. I'll make him happy because I love him and need him.

He swung the car around and stepped hard on the gas. With a free hand he switched on the radio but static jumbled the music and he turned it off again.

They reached Jack's place. Wordlessly she followed him up the musty hallway to the furnished room. Phil got the key from the ledge above the door and let them in.

He kicked the door closed and, standing in the darkness, grabbed her in his arms. She heard the soft thud as one of Jack's cats leaped off the radiator to the floor. Phil reached under her coat and pulled her to him. His hands were warm to her flesh. Her senses began to swim and she released the mounting desire she felt. Her body went limp against the insistent force of his needing. He lifted her up, carried her to the bed, and gently put her down. She felt the weight of his body on her own and soon the touch of his flesh against hers.

"I love you," she murmured. "Love you . . . love . . . you."

Her words merged with passion and the silent darkness was soon witness to their union.

2

In her own bed at last, Paula tossed fitfully, yearning for a sleep that would not come. It's all right, she kept insisting. It's all right because we're getting married. But it wasn't what she and Phil had done together that made her anxious. It was the insistent thought that soon she would have a husband, then children, and the routine of life would be carved out for her, leaving her nothing she could do to change it.

Just early yesterday, there had been nothing in the world more wonderful than to be Mrs. Carson.

Suddenly it had become important to discover who she — Paula Temple — really was. Her life, her individual self, seemed terribly precious now. Could she paint? Could she dare to be ambitious for an existence different from being Phil's wife? If Byrne hadn't looked at her like that, if Byrne hadn't said with her eyes that Paula Temple might be a person worth considering . . .

Byrne must have seen plenty of people in her time. She couldn't have looked at all of them the way she had looked at Paula.

The night dragged on. Paula sought refuge in far off stars that glittered in the eternity of the black heavens. If only she had one particle of the time those stars seemed to have!

No, she had to think of Phil.

She would be crazy not to marry him. How could you love a man one day and the next day want to run madly around the world without him? Marriage had suddenly become a trap. And that was foolish. A woman was made to get married and bear her husband's children. That was maturity, that was being an adult. The rest of life was child's play.

Then I'm a child, her mind screamed. I don't want to get married. Not yet! Not yet! I'm just beginning to live.

Once again, Paula saw those slanting eyes that ever changed color and meaning as you looked at them.

Dawn crept in. She heard Mike stir and his pillow fall to the floor. She sighed, grateful to know that soon she could get out of bed and not be alone with her thoughts for a while. Phil would call her. What would she say to him? What could she say that he would understand? She didn't understand herself what was driving her now.

Paula didn't care. She would let whatever it was force her on until some knowledge came, until she found something that made sense out of this new and frightening fascination she had never felt before. And she understood that she could not marry Phil until that happened.

She waited until seven o'clock then got out of bed. She tiptoed into her parents' room and put on her mother's robe. If only she were a kid again and could sit in that warm, comforting lap. But Paula knew that this was one problem she must solve completely alone. She pulled the bathrobe tighter around her body, wishing that it could give her the wisdom that all mothers seemed to have.

In the kitchen she sat near the stove. The peacefulness of Sunday seemed to spread itself through the world. Families would sleep until late, then read the papers and watch television in the afternoon. Some would go to church, maybe to confess their troubles. Others would visit grandparents and stuff themselves on a hearty dinner. Oh, none of it was for her now. Not for her. If only she could rip off her skin and dig out the trouble. How good it would be not to think, not to fight, not to wonder.

Her father shuffled in on his way to the bathroom, sleep still heavy in his eyes. "You up?" he mumbled. "Fight with Phil?"

"No, Pa. Just up early."

He closed the bathroom door. She heard him belch painfully.

I can't sit here all day like this. I've got to get out. Then she thought once more of Phil calling. He would tell her folks about their getting married and everyone would worry about where she had gone. No, she had to stay home until he called.

One by one, Ma and Mike and Pa got up for the day. She listened to the yawning and the brushing of teeth while she sat on the hard wood of the chair.

By eleven o'clock she was washing the dishes, letting the water scald her hands and turn the skin red. She scrubbed the plates with all the bottled-up energy surging from inside her.

Mike, too skinny for his height, his shoulders stooping awkwardly, commented to her, "You're a strange bird today."

Paula didn't answer.

Ma put on her grey Sunday dress and combed brilliantine through her hair that was supposed to smell of rose petals. "Leave your sister be," she said with merciful intuition. She smiled anxiously at her daughter and told her not to bother drying. "They can drain," she said, "if you have better things to do."

"It's all right, Ma. I'm all right."

"Of course you are."

She wished she could reassure her mother. Convince her that nothing was really wrong. But she wanted to throw her arms around that neck and cry and cry. "It's really okay, Ma," Paula insisted as she picked up the towel and started to dry. "Phil asked me to marry him last night. I guess I just don't know."

Gratefully she watched her mother's concern relax.

"Baby," she said and hugged Paula with relief. "My little baby."

She felt her mother's tears wet against her cheek

29

and her own tears came furiously, burning from somewhere deep inside.

"What the hell's goin' on in here?" Mike's disgust rang through the house.

"Oh, pipe down." His father pushed him out. "Go build yourself a hot rod."

"Aah, women!" He zipped up his jacket and slammed out of the apartment.

The old man wandered uncomfortably around the kitchen and pretended to interest himself in polishing his shoes. He brushed the tips with violent concentration.

Paula pulled herself away from her mother, aware of a throbbing in her temples. No use to cry. It solved nothing. With a paper napkin, she wiped her mother's cheeks and then her own. "I really didn't sleep much, you know. Maybe that's why things look so big this morning. I'll take an aspirin and go for a walk."

Her father said, "You want company?"

"No, Pa, thanks. I just want to clear out this head."

She found some aspirin in the medicine cabinet, bundled the scarf around her neck and pulled on her heavy mittens. She didn't much care what she looked like, even if it was Sunday. "If Phil calls, tell him — Oh, tell him anything."

She ran out and down the steps as if bursting out from under smothering blankets.

The dreary Sunday lay heavily on all the closed stores with their awnings flapping and whipping in

30

the wind. She strode down Third Avenue, coat collar turned up, head bent into the wind. The grey sky, heavy with its burden of snow, stretched endlessly above her. She walked and walked, not thinking, not wanting to think, hoping perhaps she might outrun her crazy thoughts and return to the familiar nest of long-known living.

She knew where she was walking; her legs moved without her brain's direction. I can't go there, she thought. It's nerve. It's gall. I wasn't invited. Her legs insisted, moving her block after block, seeming to gain energy and purpose as she progressed. When she had come twenty blocks to Forty Second Street, she forced herself to stop in the Woolworth doorway. If I knew her last name, she thought, I could look up her telephone. She went into a bar and searched for Byrne Carson. The name wasn't listed.

Her legs drove her outside again. They stung with the cold, but the stinging felt good as a kind of match for her rushing turmoil. She wanted to speed, to fly, to dash herself against windows. Her lips were dry from breathing through her mouth, chapped and cracked. The restless fury she felt would not let her ride the bus or take a subway. She half-ran, half-walked to Fourteenth Street, not seeing, not caring, breathing rapid painful breaths, shaking with the pounding in her heart.

At Fourteenth Street she caught sight of herself in the window of a dress store. Tangled hair and burning red cheeks stared back at her. She realized that she was in her old worn coat. Her shoes were muddy with slush. Mixed relief and horror struck her. She can't see me like this!

She had a ready-made excuse just to stand across

the street from Byrne's house and watch the window. Maybe she would come to fix a curtain. As Paula considered this, the idea became increasingly appealing. She hurried to Eleventh Street, practically convinced that she had an appointment to glimpse Byrne at the window.

When she spotted the house, her pace slowed. To see the building better she stayed on the opposite side of the street. At last she stood directly across, glutting herself with staring at the strange but so familiar door. A glow spread inside her as she realized that somewhere, right behind this thin piece of glass, was that golden hair splashed with fire — that vibrant voice that could laugh and softly caress at the same time. She leaned back against ice-covered bricks, feeling warm and touched with peace.

How long she stood, Paula didn't know. Her eyes strained with a permanent watching of the window for fear that if she glanced away for even a second, she might miss the sight of Byrne. Perhaps she was reading, lying casually on the couch, her legs crossed on the cushions, a drink on the table beside her.

Paula's coat had soaked in the wetness and a freezing bar of dampness cut across her back. She shivered. Her fingers inside the mittens had become stiff and she tried to move them to stir the circulation.

What would Byrne think if she happened to knock on her door?

If I don't go all the way in, Paula thought, if I just stand inside the front door for awhile, she'll never know. Still hesitating, she shifted her weight to the other foot. A prickling sensation ran through her toes. Her feet seemed like two blocks of wood on which she rocked, unable to sense the movement of walking. Yes, I'll go inside, she thought. Maybe I'll hear her voice on the telephone, or something.

With quick decision she stumbled across the street, moving clumsily on frozen limbs. She crept slowly up the steps, watching the window in case Byrne might appear. She needed both thumbs to push the door latch down and she slipped quickly inside, closing the door carefully so it wouldn't bang.

A puddle formed around her shoes and gradually the heat of indoors thawed her fingers. She pushed the scarf back off her head so that her ears would be free to hear any sound behind the door. So close. So close.

It might have been five minutes, it might have been a half hour that she waited, smiling crazily at the knocker, dizzily scared that Byrne might come out and find her. Footsteps came down the staircase. An old gentleman in rimless glasses looked at her with questioning eyes. He tipped his hat.

"May I help you?" he said.

"No, thank you," she answered quickly, "I'm just waiting for someone."

"I see." He smiled and went out.

But that did it. The man had hardly closed the door when Byrne's door opened. She poked her head out and saw Paula.

"Voices carry around here," she said around a black cigarette holder clamped between her teeth. She didn't seem so much surprised as amused. "If you're waiting for someone," a glint of mockery flicked in her eyes, "you'll be a little more comfortable waiting in here."

Paula's heart dropped right down to her stomach.

She didn't move. Mixtures of horror and joy scrambled inside her.

"Well, come in before we both freeze to death." Byrne leaned into the hall and pulled the girl back into her apartment.

Unlike yesterday's neatness, the room was full of half empty coffee cups. They littered the floor, the table, the book shelf. And Byrne wore a striped shirt, the sleeves rolled past the elbow, with the same charcoal slacks and sandals.

"My God, you're an ice cube. Have you been out there all night?" Indulgence tempered her irony.

Paula laughed suddenly at her own foolishness. It's so simple, she thought. I'm here! And there was not the slightest feeling of intrusion.

"Well, if you can't talk, perhaps you can take off those wet things."

Submissively Paula removed her coat and dropped herself on the couch. She felt light with happiness, not caring if Byrne thought she were a fool.

"At least you're not making excuses. Take off your shoes while I get you some hot coffee."

Paula watched her stoop to the automatic percolator plugged in beside the wall lamp. She liked the starkness of Byrne today. It made the grace of her body and movements more apparent by contrast.

"I hate to wash cups," Byrne chatted with offhand friendliness. "We have three more to go before it's necessary."

"Don't waste a clean one," Paula said. "Please just fill that one there."

"Child, how can you be so natural?"

Paula leaned back on the couch and devoured the

beautiful thing that was Byrne. "I guess I can't help it."

Byrne filled one of the used cups and brought it over. "No, I guess you can't."

Paula took the steaming cupful and sipped from it. She really didn't know why Byrne thought it was so natural to drink from a used cup. But the thought that Byrne noticed it, had held it, had touched it to her own lips, made Paula lazily linger with her tongue over the rim.

Byrne sat on the edge of the couch and unlaced Paula's shoes. She dropped them to the floor and massaged the cold feet. "If you die of pneumonia, Phil will never forgive me."

She abandoned herself to Byrne's attentions, hoping her feet would stay cold forever so that the warm strong fingers would always be touching her. "He doesn't know I'm here," she sighed. "Nobody knows."

"Do you like secrets? I wouldn't have thought so."

Paula didn't know how to explain that this wasn't a secret, exactly. It was more precious than a secret, this day. It was like a delicate infant that she didn't want strangers to breathe on. She put the cup down on the floor and surrendered to a drowsiness that flowed upward from Byrne's moving fingers.

"Byrne," she said, "Byrne, tell me why I'm here."

Abruptly the woman released Paula's feet. She ran her fingers in the familiar gesture through the back of her hair and moved away from the couch. She stood looking down at Paula and Paula had the odd sensation of being measured for an unknown role.

"It's not important," Byrne said casually and brought a flaring match to meet her cigarette.

"Isn't it?"

"No. You are simply growing up. Remember how important your breasts were when you first noticed them? Now they're something you take for granted. They don't rule you."

Paula didn't understand. But if Byrne said it wasn't important, she would have to believe her. And yet a peculiar substance seemed to hang in the room, as though a voice were speaking not quite loud enough to be heard.

"Maybe I'm here because I want to paint," she mused, wanting to capture and to understand. "I never realized that a woman's body could be so inspiring." She looked up at the picture. "Will you show me how?"

"Why not? I think there are some sketch pads in the bedroom," Byrne answered with almost scientific directness, "if you'd like your first lesson now."

Paula heard her rummaging through drawers. She wondered what kind of bed Byrne slept in. Did she sleep alone? The accomplishment of being here gave Paula courage. She got up and went to see what the room where Byrne spent her nights was like.

She leaned against the doorway and saw a strange-looking double bed. The mahogany headboard rose elaborately into carved angels and rosebuds. It didn't look as if it should be Byrne's bed. It seemed more the kind of thing that grandparents slept in. Byrne, reaching to a top shelf in the closet, did not notice Paula's inspection. Nor did she see the girl approach the cigarette box on the dressing table.

Paula looked at it curiously. A woman's

photograph had been inserted in the center and covered by a curving glass that magnified the face. A face that pouted sadly, with delicate, unpainted lips trying a smile for the camera. The blonde hair, so blonde that it looked white, came in wisps of bangs over the forehead. The eyes seemed to dream of distant visions. Paula didn't like the face. It held a sense of evil, and frightened her.

"Here it is," Byrne said, stepping back from the closet and dusting off a spiral pad. "What's the matter?"

"Who is this?" Paula's voice was hardly audible.

"Oh, what do you care. Is there a pencil on the dresser top?"

But Paula couldn't take her eyes away from the face. It held her with its almost innocent wickedness.

"Since you must know, she is the artist you so much admired. But don't let it upset you. That picture was taken many years ago. She's even older than I am."

Paula whirled. "You're not old. I wish you would stop saying that. You're young and you'll stay that way until the end — until the end of the earth. Only sick people get old. And poor miserable creatures who want to run away from what they are!"

Byrne examined her with mixed concern and enjoyment. Laugh lines wrinkled into the freckles across her nose. "One would never guess you had it in you," she said. "Now will you forget that picture and let's get down to business?"

For the first time, Paula realized how rude she was being. Her cheeks warmed and she dropped her glance to the carpet. "I'm sorry. I really shouldn't have come in here."

"Never mind. You're a person who has to discover things the hard way. I'm only trying to make it a little easier for you if I can."

"Well, I haven't discovered a thing. I don't understand at all why you're so good to me." She searched Byrne for an answer and found only those ocean-green eyes washing her with silence.

The woman firmly steered her out of the bedroom and back into the other world.

She set up a portable easel beside the bookshelf and stood the pad on it.

"Now, start with something simple. Try that percolator for instance."

Obediently, Paula sketched the percolator. She felt no shyness about drawing. The old confidence from school reflected in her fingers. She drew the picture large with generous shading. Then she drew a cup and saucer with the percolator. Byrne stood behind her, offering no comment.

"Do I make your nervous if I watch?"

"Oh, no. I like you near me." Intent on her work, Paula hardly knew the meaning of what she said. Page after page she filled with chairs and trees and fruit bowls.

Byrne finally said, "I wonder how well you sketch from life."

"I never did."

"Let's try. I'll be your model."

Without embarrassment, as though it were the most everyday thing in the world, Byrne unbuttoned her shirt and dropped it to the floor. Paula watched, speechless, as she unhooked her bra and tossed it aside. The girl's sight traveled over the smooth shoulders and down the arms. Byrne perched herself

38

on the arm of the couch and said, "All right, draw." There was no hint of challenge in her voice. It was matter of fact and sensible.

Paula clutched her pencil and stabbed grimly at the paper in front of her. The lines trembled as she drew them. She clenched her teeth, desperately trying to concentrate on the picture. Struggling for control, she managed neck and shoulders. With great detail, she drew the hands, the fingers crossed on the lap. She worked over the wrist bones half a dozen times to get them properly. Then up to the hollow in the throat. She examined her work and realized how ridiculous it looked. The middle was all blank. I can't stare at her breasts like that, she thought. But I've got to. It means nothing. She expects me to do my best. Why am I acting like such a . . .

Taking a deep breath, she forced herself to look at that forbidden area. The pencil froze in her hand. Imploringly, she searched Byrne's face, but the expression there remained impersonal. At last she got the pencil to the paper and sketched a few quick lines to indicate the feminine softness. Perspiration beaded across her forehead as she forced the pencil on and on over the page.

"All right," she grunted. "I've finished now."

"Good." Byrne hopped off the couch and strolled over, not bothering to put on her shirt again.

Her nakedness loomed so close to Paula. The girl became dizzy and stepped backward. "Please," she whispered, "put on your shirt." She couldn't bear looking at the body. But her eyes wouldn't leave the incredible beauty of those twin shapes that to her seemed to be glowing in the lamplight.

Byrne didn't move to get her clothing. "It's only

art," she murmured. "If you want to draw, you can't be so personal."

Paula twisted away and stared at the wall. "Please," she groaned. "Please." She heard Byrne's tongue click with impatience.

"All right," she said after a moment's pause. "I'm decent now. You can look." Her voice mocked the girl.

Shame crept into Paula as she realized she had revealed an odd modesty. Normal women undressed before each other without concern, without embarrassment. She turned to face the woman and ask forgiveness for the strange demon that clawed inside her.

"Don't apologize," Byrne stopped her. "If you'd rather draw cups and saucers the rest of your life, you're welcome to it."

"Do you strip that way for everyone?" Paula asked.

"No. Of course not."

"Did *she* see you naked?"

"Oh, my heavens! What do you want, a life history? Yes, Greta saw me naked. She diapered me and changed my bathing suit at the seashore. She slept in that bed, if you must know. And sometimes she still does, God help her. I told you I wasn't young."

Byrne got out the scotch and poured herself a stiff drink.

"Give me one, too," Paula said.

"Not on your life. You'll get drunk and bawl at me about how pure you thought all this was."

"Pure? I'm not pure, either," Paula lashed out. "I went to bed with Phil last night. It was the most miserable and disgusting thing that ever happened to me. I felt as if my insides were being torn to shreds. And that's supposed to be love. Oh, I'm a slut just like everybody else. You don't have to worry." Shaken by her explosion of frankness, Paula grabbed the bottle and splashed whiskey into a cup.

"If you drink that," Byrne said, her voice low, the words chiseled, "you're never to come back here again."

Paula stood glaring at her, the cup uncertainly poised.

Never to see Byrne again!

The demon put its fingers around her neck and pressed until she couldn't swallow. Slowly, she lowered the cup. I'd rather die, she thought.

"That's better," Byrne relaxed. "Now come over here and sit down."

Without question, Paula went. There was nothing she would not do if only Byrne could be pleased with her again.

"You draw quite well." Byrne resumed her teaching manner. "But it's obvious that you need lots of practice. Do you think you can control yourself for a couple of weeks until you master the fundamentals?"

"Yes," Paula said, not knowing whether she could or not. "I can do anything you think is necessary."

"Good. Now, you're too upset to go any farther today. Suppose you come back Tuesday evening. I'll have better supplies by then."

Paula didn't want to leave, but she knew the woman had other things to do than dawdle with her. Regretfully, she put on her coat.

"Here's cab fare home." Byrne tilted Paula's chin.

"And don't think about this too much. If I didn't like you, I wouldn't take the trouble."

Paula felt a beaming smile leap to her face. Byrne pressed a five dollar bill into her hand and pushed her out the door.

She skipped dizzily up the street. She likes me! She likes me no matter what I did!

At the corner of Fifth Avenue, she hailed a cab. Once inside, she crossed her legs and tried to sit like a lady. It wasn't often that she could ride like this. What wonderful, marvelous things would Byrne make possible for her? If she could only return some of the joy, some of the gratefulness that filled her. She resolved that anything Byrne asked her to do — sketch her nude, anything — she would do it if it took all the courage she could muster. She would please Byrne. She must please Byrne. Nothing in life was so important as Byrne's approval.

The cabbie changed the five dollars and raised his eyebrows when she told him to keep the change.

3

Paula burst into the apartment and ran to her room, anxious to be alone with her dreaming. It was hardly four o'clock and the smell of roast chicken reminded her that she hadn't eaten all day.

Her mother came into her room and waited until Paula had taken off her things.

"Phil was here," she said. "He waited for you an hour and a half." Her voice held a question.

"Didn't you tell him I was out?"

"Yes. But he expected that you would be back soon."

The idea of Phil returned to Paula like an old shoe, suddenly found. She wished he would stay, like an old shoe, in the closet and wait until she was ready for him.

"Maybe you'd better call him," her mother offered. She was wearing an apron over the Sunday dress. The family hadn't gone out today. Uncomfortably, Paula supposed they were worrying about her.

"All right, I'll call him. After dinner." She didn't want to speak to Phil. He would ask where she'd been. Now that he had proposed, he probably felt a right to question her. Could she put him off without making him angry? Perhaps. But not without hurting him. Oh, she seemed to be hurting everybody. Ma and Pa this afternoon and now Phil.

"I only spent a harmless afternoon," Paula explained, "away from troubles. There's nothing wrong with that, is there?"

Her mother looked at the pencil smudges on her fingers. "If you're feeling better, I'm glad you went wherever it was."

"I'm feeling fine," Paula almost sang. If only I could tell you about it! The faint odor of pomade lingered as her mother went to light the stove under the cold chicken.

Why can't I tell her, she thought. What's wrong with what I've done? But she didn't want to speak about her dear Byrne. The thought of Byrne in this apartment didn't fit. She wasn't the kind of person you discussed in cold water flats. Not even to your mother. Byrne was meant for dreaming late at night. Late at night in the dark and all alone.

She changed into a pair of corduroy slacks and

44

looked at herself in the bubbles of the mirror that framed the old dressing table. She didn't have those trim lines. Her hips were too rounded, her waist too small. She searched out one of Mike's old shirts and jammed the tails into her trousers. Then she rolled up the too-long sleeves and once more examined her reflection. She just wasn't impressive.

The mound of mashed potatoes and gravy added strength to her unwound nerves. Halfway through the meal the phone rang. Pa was taking a nap in the bedroom. She and her mother looked at each other.

"If it's Phil, tell him I'm eating and he can pick me up at seven."

Paula knew she would have to see him. No matter how much she didn't want to, it was better to get this over with soon. Or he would be calling and wondering and having fits.

"Don't you want to talk to him?" Ma tried to cover her perplexity.

"Not just now." Paula attended to the chicken.

She listened to her mother deliver the message while she poured vinegar into the almost empty bottle of ketchup.

"He'll be over," her mother said, setting a dish of fruit salad on the table.

Well, she didn't have to think about Phil until he got here. Some excuse would come to her by then. She didn't care to lie to him. But he would never understand the truth. What was the truth? She hardly knew herself. All she knew was that this afternoon was her own private possession.

Phil arrived almost promptly at seven, his features muddled with concern. She motioned him to a chair and he sat on it sideways because his long legs wouldn't fit comfortably under the table. She could tell he wanted to talk to her earnestly but he made polite conversation for the sake of her mother.

At last he said, "Want to catch a movie?"

Her eyesight was strained from the afternoon's sketching, but she agreed just to get them out of the house.

They didn't go to the movies, of course. He took her to Jack's place.

"Look," he said, when they had closed the door, "I didn't do anything — I mean, it was all right?"

She considered the appeal in his eyes, then the yellow rumpled bedsheets. The musty smell of stale furniture and cat hairs over everything curdled her stomach.

"Sure," she said. "It was all right."

The sound of Whitey scratching in the kitty litter filled the silence. A pot of left-over spaghetti filled with water sat in the wash basin. "No, it wasn't all right," she blurted. "It's miserable here and I hate it. Why do we always have to come to this place? Why couldn't you have waited until we had somewhere decent?"

He looked at her with confusion. She saw the irritation growing within him and the line of his mouth tightened. "You're a strange girl today. I can't believe it was all my fault."

Immediately she felt sorry for him. After all, he was battling against something he didn't even know about. She couldn't help him. She could hardly help herself, let alone Phil.

"If I'm so strange, then just leave me be." The hardness in Paula's voice covered her own groping to understand.

"Oh, honey, why don't you come off it? That was bound to happen sooner or later. What difference could it make that we didn't have a license for it last night?"

There was no point in arguing. How can you explain to a man, still dear to you, he has suddenly been replaced?

"The fact is, Phil, I'm not sure that I'm ready to get married just yet."

"And why not? You seemed plenty eager these past couple of months."

That was the truth and it slapped her. She went to open a window, thinking some fresh air might chase the musty smell. She opened the window and thought: If I jumped out all this mess would be over. She stood looking down the narrow alleyway at the empty clotheslines tangled from the wind.

"I know I owe you an explanation, but the truth is I haven't any."

"Sure, you haven't. You don't know what in hell you're talking about. When they say women are addle-brained, I have an idea this is exactly what they mean."

He was being nasty. But it was nastiness out of desperation, she knew. He had to fight back against this unknown enemy. If he fought clumsily, it was nonetheless brave.

"Phil, I love you. I just need time to work something over in my mind. Will you try to be patient and not force me?"

"Patient? God save us all! Here I am planning for our marriage next month and you say to be patient. Is that what you call love?"

"All right, then," she challenged. A stabbing

47

frustration and restlessness shot through. "Call it off. Go away and leave me alone. I don't want to see you, Phil. I want to be alone. Do you hear me? Alone!"

He grabbed her away from the window and pulled her beside him against the wall. "You're nuts," his voice rasped. "Stark, raving nuts."

She struggled, pounding his chest with clenched fists. "Leave me be!" she shouted. "Leave me be!"

He held her fast. "You're going to calm down and straighten out." Grabbing her wrists, he held them fast behind her back. "Honey, you're hysterical."

Twisting and turning, she tried to free herself from his grasp. Biting at his arm, she caught the material of his shirt between her teeth and ripped it.

His bulk was too much for her. Panting, she let her body collapse. For a moment he stood supporting the weight of her in his arms. Then slowly, she slipped to the floor and collapsed at his feet. He kneeled beside her, not knowing what to do. She crawled over, put her head in his lap and sobbed wretchedly.

Clumsily, he stroked her hair. "It's all right, honey. If you want to be alone, it's okay." His voice was heavy with sadness. "Just don't get lost," he said. "We need each other too much."

When he brought her home, he didn't try to kiss her. He sort of patted her shoulder and ran off down the steps. She listened to the disappearing jingle of his house keys.

Paula was grateful for Monday. Getting up and yelling at Mike to hurry up out of the bathroom kept

48

her from thinking for the moment about the strange state of affairs in her life.

The rush hour crowds carried her down the steps to the subway where she stood on line to buy a week's supply of tokens.

Her office friends greeted her and chatted about their dates as if this had been a weekend like any other. Paula felt as though she had been away for a hundred years until her desk, her typewriter, the small switchboard with its tails and plugs hypnotized her back into the meaningless routine.

At five o'clock she looked for Phil's car but it wasn't there. She waited ten minutes. He didn't show up. She realized with huge relief that he really was going to let her alone for awhile. Poor guy. She didn't like herself very much for yesterday's scene, but as she tried to think of Phil, the picture of him faded, replaced by the image of that shirtless body, the tantalizing curves of warm flesh, coldly posed for sketching.

When she got home, the place was jammed with Mike's friends making a pretense of doing homework. Pa hadn't arrived yet. She helped set the table and prepared a place for him, even though she didn't know whether or not he would be in any condition to eat.

Ma said, "Did you have a good day?"

"Like every other," Paula answered. Then she said, "Ma, did you think when you got married that this was the way life was going to be?"

Her mother wiped her hands on the apron and studied the worn wedding ring on her finger. "That's a funny question, my dear. In those days, you know, we didn't think about how it would all turn out. We

49

just took our chances. We trusted the man to do what he should do, and so would we." She always spoke in terms of "we" because she had seven sisters.

"But didn't you have any imagination? Didn't you wonder whether the future was going to be bright or not?"

"Maybe old-fashioned people take it for granted the future will be bright. I guess I don't know, dear."

Paula knew her mother wasn't trying to chide her. And she was being discreet enough not to ask why Phil hadn't brought her home. He always came upstairs for a short visit. Her mother enjoyed the company. She liked Phil. And Paula could see that her own sudden hesitance about marrying him was a disappointment.

The boys were fighting so loudly over the verb of a sentence that nobody heard Pa come in. He stumbled into the kitchen and fell heavily on the table, his face yellow with a frightening pallor.

"Harry!" Her mother ran to him. He fell forward, upsetting the empty glasses, and lay with his cheek against the oilcloth.

Paula ran to the phone to call the doctor. Her hands trembled as they dialed numbers.

She cleared the boys out and sent Mike with them. Her father lay at the table, retching with spasms, speechless in pain. She and her mother tried to move him to the bed but he couldn't make it.

The doctor arrived, and the three of them managed to get the old man into bed. After the examination, the doctor put his stethoscope in his bag and filled out a prescription.

"It's nothing to worry about, Mrs. Temple. He'll have to stay in bed for a couple of weeks. No alcohol, of course. Plenty of tea and broth and rest. This will keep him quiet through the night. I'll drop by tomorrow."

Paula gave him the five dollar visiting fee, regretting the generous tip to the cabbie yesterday. Every penny she earned was tightly accounted for. Doctor bills were things to be dreaded. They could cut a hole into your life that sometimes took years to repair. Nothing to worry about, the doctor said. Well, there was plenty to worry about.

She put her lunch money into a pocket and went to the drugstore. Luckily, the pills cost only a couple of dollars but there weren't many in the small glass vial. If Pa needed a new supply every day, she would have to start taking sandwiches to work.

She came back upstairs glumly, trying to muster a smile as she entered the apartment. Her mother was just coming out of the bedroom, the weight of her concern obvious in the dark pockets under her eyes.

Paula said, "It'll be okay. At least we don't have any babies to worry about. Mike's sixteen. It won't hurt him to take a job for a while."

"You're a good girl." The tone of her mother's voice made Paula feel that she herself was a baby with good intentions, but one who didn't really understand.

This wasn't the time to convince Ma about Mike. She dropped the subject and got a glass of water to take with the pills to Pa.

Limp with nausea and pain, her father lay beneath the covers. You could tell the pain was bad from the way his fingers were twisted. He looked small and shriveled. What little of his strength she could remember had long ago drained away. Nothing inside the white skin, crepe-like over pale blue veins. She unwrapped the bottle and tried not to look at him. Tried not to think how things would be if Pa died.

She helped him to sit up. She put two pills directly into his mouth rather than go through the agony of watching those weakened fingers struggle. He sipped enough water to get them down and gasped for breath.

"They'll put you to sleep," she comforted.

He was too ill to attempt a smile and she wished she could rush from the room to escape the nightmare of her father's sickness. Instead, she tucked the covers around his shoulders and asked if there was anything he wanted. The brown eyes, dull with their misery, closed to say no. Paula switched out the lights and went back into the kitchen.

Her heart turned over to see her mother sitting helplessly at the table, staring into space.

"He's going to sleep," Paula said. "Maybe I'd better get Mike for supper." She had to keep things going. Life had to keep on going, no matter what happened. Besides, she couldn't really believe that Pa was going to die. You get used to having a person around and it's just not conceivable that all of a sudden he would stop being there. Sure, he'd be sick for a while. Plenty sick. But he would get better. He had to.

Even so, Paula knew that it was her duty to take charge. Her job alone would have to support them all. Her strength alone would hold the family together. She felt terribly little and she wanted Ma to tell her everything would be all right, but Ma was sitting there, worn out and exhausted from the years of constant struggle.

"If you can get supper started," Paula repeated, "I'll be back with Mike just as soon as I find him."

Once again, she got her coat and left the house. She had to ignore the knot of aching nerves in her head. Her neck ached too, with the tension. Actually, she didn't know where Mike would be. Maybe over at one of the other boy's homes. She reached the street, undecided which way to go but she had to do something, had to keep moving. She couldn't just stand there and be defeated without any kind of fight. So she went first to the corner candy store, hoping some of the boys might be hanging around.

She looked inside. The stools were empty. It was after six o'clock. Everybody was probably home eating supper, just as she would be if things were as they always were.

Maybe she should go to the clubhouse. It was half a dozen blocks down the street at the Lennox Settlement. She looked into the pingpong room and asked some of the kids. Nobody had seen Mike. Paula felt herself getting irritated. Mike should have had the decency not to hide himself at a time like this. Paula thought he should be grown up enough by now not to cause more trouble on top of all the trouble they already had. She found a pay phone and called Charlie, Mike's best friend. No, Mike hadn't come home with him. No, he didn't know where Mike might be.

Paula slammed down the receiver and went back into the streets, feeling ready to scream. She strode around the block, peering into stores and bars, thinking she might run into him accidentally. Oh, she wasn't about to spend the night chasing after her fool brother. Then, for no good reason, she thought of phoning Phil. Maybe it was force of habit.

Phil answered the ring. His deep, long and drawn "hello" brought a catch to her throat.

"Oh, Phil," she said, knowing he no longer expected her to explain about the other night. "I'm looking for Mike. Have you seen him, by any chance?"

Miraculously, because Phil had always solved her troubles, he helped her now. Yes, he had seen Mike. In fact, he was there now but he didn't want to go home. He didn't want to speak to her, either. She could come over and try to talk to him if she wanted, but he was not in any mood for the big sister act.

She thanked him and with relief hung up the phone. There wasn't time to think about the strangeness in Phil's voice. The peculiar coldness that made her feel she had put him behind bars. Things would have to be all right with Phil. Eventually she could straighten things out. This just wasn't the time. If anything, she was more confused and undecided than before.

The bus took her over to Phil's house. He answered the door with a curt nod, hands jammed tightly into the pockets of the fatigue pants streaked with car grease.

Mike was sprawled in the easy chair, slugging down beer from a can. She had never seen Mike drink before. She wondered whether this was the first time or if he had been doing it all along behind everyone's back. The apartment smelled of that pungent beer odor. She realized that it wasn't just the house, it was Phil. Both he and Mike had been drinking.

"Look, Mike," she said, "we need you at home." It was a direct appeal. She spoke as one adult to another.

Mike didn't look at her. He stared sullenly at the fishing pole propped in a corner of the room.

"Pa's going to be in bed a couple of weeks. We'll all have to put our heads together about what has to be done."

Still no answer. He swung one sneakered foot, emphasizing the feigned indifference and outrage that consumed him. Phil had flopped down on the sofa and crossed his hands behind his head. He didn't interfere but lay still as though trying to make himself invisible.

"Why in hell are you being so stubborn?" Paula's voice rose. "I tell you we're in trouble. You've got to come home."

"Yeah," Mike said, his voice thick. "You need me. You all need me like a hole in the head."

"Oh, behave, for Pete's sake," Paula clasped her fingers together with impatience. "Are you going to be sensitive now because I pushed your friends out?"

"You pushed *me* out." He glared at her. Patches of beard roughened his smooth skin.

How was she going to convince him? There wasn't time to explain the facts of life to him now, not with Ma home by herself.

"All right," Paula gave in. "So I pushed you out. It's just one of those things."

"So it happened. So now I'm going to stay away. Phil and me both. We're not a couple of dummies that dance when you say we should."

She looked at Phil. He didn't come to her defense.

"So that's the way it is?" she said. "You're going to sit here and feel sorry for yourself. You won't help out."

"It if doesn't suit your convenience, that's too damned bad."

I'm arguing with the alcohol, she decided, not Mike. "Okay, stay here as long as you want. But remember, Pa's out of work and I don't bring home enough to keep things going. If you don't get a job after school, I don't know how we'll manage."

He took a long slug from the can and swallowed with a grimace of distaste. A thin line of foam clung to the shadow of his mustache. "That's tough," he said.

There wasn't anything she could do. She wheeled and stalked out, hating Phil for not helping her in the slightest. Surely he understood what was happening. Even if she had hurt him, he could be big enough to overlook it in this case. He felt very much like Mike, probably. Unwanted. Unneeded. So they teamed up against her. It was too ridiculous.

By the time she got home, Ma had pulled herself together. Two portions of ham and eggs were waiting. Paula knew that Ma was too sick inside herself to have an appetite. She had fixed dinner for only Paula and Mike.

Seeing Paula alone, her fine dark eyebrows came together in question.

"I found him," Paula volunteered. "He's over at Phil's place and he doesn't want to come home."

"Did you really expect something different?" She put a single serving on the table.

"Yes. I expected him to act like an adult."

"Well, eat your supper. He'll calm down by tomorrow. Don't worry about it."

Paula sat down and played with the fork. Her own appetite was gone but she knew she should try to eat. "I'm not worried. I'm disgusted. He's sixteen years old."

"Weren't you?"

It was an unfair reply. She was working so hard to be brave and keep things organized and even her own mother wasn't helping. She pushed a piece of bread into her mouth and chewed it slowly. The whole world was ganging up on her. Phil thought she was a traitor. Mike was living in a fog of hurt feelings more important to him than anyone's life or death. And here was Ma taking everybody's side but hers. The supper was going down in lumps. She forced herself to keep on eating.

Mike didn't come home that night. Paula paced around her room, cursing his stubbornness. She felt trapped and miserable. Wasn't there anyone who could understand her feelings? She climbed into bed and dug her face into the pillow. The memory of patient warm fingers massaging the cold flesh of her feet swept through her. She saw the freckles crinkling with laughter across the nose, the steaming coffee offered to warm her.

Oh, Byrne, she whispered, take me away!

4

All through Tuesday, Paula fought to stay calm. She had to type letters three and four times to get them right. Her fingers refused to move sanely on the keys. They leaped and jumped and stumbled unmanageably. The girls, usually so talkative, started conversations with her but soon drifted away, sensing that Paula was in no mood for light chatter.

She hadn't bothered to take lunch along. When twelve o'clock came, she went to the coffee machine in the cafeteria and drowned herself in gallons of black liquid. She knew she was tired under everything but the blood raced through her veins and her mind sped dizzily along its crazy channel of thought.

How could she leave the house tonight and go to Byrne? What excuse could she give Ma for deserting her?

She had to see Byrne. She couldn't stay in that hopeless apartment, caged by those dismal surroundings. Byrne, cool Byrne, flowed like clear water through the desert of her life. She would rather die than not go tonight.

She lit a cigarette from the stub of another and put her head in her hands. Around her the chatter and clinking of dishes went unnoticed.

I don't know her last name, she thought. I can't phone her and explain why I can't come.

Instantly she thought of phoning Phil and asking him. Then she rejected the idea. Even if he didn't ask, Phil would want to know why. He might get in touch with Byrne to find out what was going on.

The afternoon dragged on with its usual businesslike boredom. The round clock on the wall ticked but its hands didn't seem to move. Paula lived a hundred years before five o'clock arrived.

When Paula came home, the doctor had already paid his visit. She noticed that there were no more pills in the bottle. Then she saw another bottle with different colored tablets standing behind the bedlamp. Pa lay sleeping. He breathed in long, slow breaths and she didn't have to ask her mother if he was drugged. He looked thinner than ever and more colorless than a piece of paper. A bowl of broth, almost full, sat on the floor beside his bed. There was nothing for Paula to say to her mother. They moved their own silent ways through the stillness of the apartment.

When she had washed her face and renewed the lipstick, Paula felt a little better. She knew she was going to Byrne tonight. It was senseless to stay home anyway. What could she do to help? If Pa was up and needed attention, that would be one thing. But as long as he slept, Paula felt free to leave for a few hours.

Her mother noticed the fresh lipstick. "Don't you want any supper?" she asked.

"I'm not hungry," Paula answered. "Has Mike been home?"

"No. But I spoke to him on the phone. I think he'll be through sulking pretty soon. Will you please try not to make him feel like a baby when he does come home?"

"I just don't see why you allow him to go around like that without having him help out at all."

"He told me Phil is going to get him a part-time job in the paint store."

"Well, that's a little better," Paula said, grateful that Ma didn't reply with an I-told-you-so.

"Since you're going out, I suppose I should tell Phil when he comes up not to wait?"

So, Paula thought with irritation, he's trying to patch things up behind my mother's apron.

As she thought that, Paula felt guilty. After all, the situation was not Phil's fault. He was simply trying not to be objectionable. She knew he was wondering what he had done wrong, questioning himself, searching, regretting what had happened that

60

night. Poor, dear Phil. He would never know that the wrongdoing, the fault, was not his.

"Yes," she said, "tell him not to wait. He has no business expecting me to be home whenever he thinks I ought to be."

"You usually are home, my dear. You've always been home during the week."

Paula realized that even if she didn't owe Phil an explanation, she owed her mother one. The faith that underlined her mother's words to her was precious. Any other mother would demand to know where her daughter had suddenly started spending time. But her mother trusted her. Paula yearned to be worthy of that trust.

"Believe me," Paula said, as she checked the contents of her purse, "I'm not doing anything you would be ashamed of. I simply have a new friend. It's right to make friends."

"You don't have to explain. I know that I've brought up a good, sensible girl."

Impulsively, Paula kissed the plump cheeks, then quickly left, before their conversation became an agony.

Once free in the winter-dark streets, the weight of her home dropped away and Paula flew with light feet over to Fifth Avenue. The thought of Byrne flooded through her body, lending it strength, life, joy, and she succumbed completely to the delightful vision of her new world. She didn't care if she was early for her appointment. If Byrne was eating supper, if Byrne was doing anything, she would sit in a corner and wait. Wait throughout eternity so long as Byrne was near.

61

She took the brownstone steps two at a time and knocked vigorously at the door. When it opened, she stood there, grinning like a maniac at the cameo face, so near to her at last.

"And what's so funny," Byrne said, tugging Paula inside by the collar. She wore a turtleneck sweater of dark green that make her eyes seem stormy. The cable stitching outlined the fullness of her breasts.

Oh, take that sweater off, Paula thought. Let me draw them. Paint them. Let me see!

The beige skirt surprised her. For the first time, it occurred to Paula that Byrne didn't always stay at home, that she had a life outside. Paula must get to know that life. She must know everything about Byrne.

"I'm laughing," Paula said, dropping her coat on a chair, "because I don't even know your last name."

"You know other things that are much more interesting," Byrne replied. The high heels she wore lent a certain formality to her. Paula had expected the same intimacy they had shared last time to reappear automatically but Byrne seemed preoccupied. She refused to sit down, as though expecting another, more important, visitor. She played with the ring on her finger and occasionally glanced out the window. Anxiety wrinkled her forehead.

"Byrne, am I intruding tonight?" An uncomfortable wedge of jealousy slid through Paula. She suddenly felt a demand for all of Byrne's attention.

"No, no," Byrne answered quickly. She patted the girl's hand. "Just one minute. I have something for you." She walked swiftly into the other room and returned with a large wrapped package. "See what I brought you?"

Paula took the brown paper off and revealed a set of charcoal pencils, and india-ink pen, half a dozen sketch pads of different sizes. Paula smiled her appreciation, but her only thought was that she mustn't waste Byrne's time. She would get right to work.

The easel stood in its place. Paula set the largest of the pads on it. "Going to pose for me?"

The old grin spread across Byrne's features. "Are you braver tonight?"

"Oh, much," Paula nodded with enthusiasm. She wasn't at all brave but this was one way to get Byrne out of those horribly conventional and covering clothes.

Byrne dragged a chair across the room and sat down, turning her profile to Paula.

Paula hesitated. She stared at Byrne for a while, waiting for some inspiration to move her pencil. "I liked it better the other way," she said in a small voice, not daring to look at Byrne.

She heard a laugh rumble out of the woman. It seemed to lap around Paula, dissolving her conviction — and her confidence.

"Well, it's true." Paula's voice shook. She could not stop the fierceness of the pride and the honesty demanding freedom. "You have the most beautiful body I ever saw. Why don't you take off your clothes? Do you want me to draw properly?" Her cheeks flushed with passion.

"Don't get excited," Byrne replied mildly. "If you prefer me nude, I have no objections."

With deliberate movement, she stood up. Slowly, she kicked off one shoe, then the other, her glance fixed on Paula. She pulled the zipper down and let her skirt slide to the floor.

Paula saw the white nylon of Byrne's slip and the outline of garters beneath. She's going to go all the way, Paula thought frantically. I've got to stay calm, I've got to stay calm.

Wordlessly, with a hint of a cynical smile flitting across her lips, Byrne pulled the sweater over her head, revealing the hollows of her cleanly shaven armpits. The warm odor of her perfumed body floated on the air. She dropped the sweater carelessly and started to raise her slip. Paula clutched the easel, paralyzed by the thing that was happening to her. Her stomach contracted with waves of unfamiliar sensation she could not name.

Byrne reached behind and unhooked the white garter belt that encircled her flat stomach. She undid the stockings and moved them with both thumbs down the length of thigh and calf. Then, not hurrying, she discarded her bra, freeing the firm curves of her breasts. With one final movement, she stepped out of her panties and stood full face to Paula.

"Is this what you want?" she asked. Her voice was soft and tense.

Paula released her hold on the easel and remained firmly planted on her own two feet. The loveliness before her gave the girl sudden clear thought. As though she had emerged from a long dark hall into the sunlight, she stood shining with the knowledge of her own motives. Byrne's body was no longer a confusing challenge; her flesh was a goal to be somehow reached.

"Yes," Paula answered, and put the pencil down.

Drawn by her need, Paula approached that body and leaned forward to brush her lips against the bare flesh.

Byrne grasped her shoulders and held her firmly at arm's length. "Do you know what you're doing?" she asked.

"No. And I don't care." She fought out of Byrne's grasp and grasped at the sweet compelling curves. Together, they fell to the couch. Paula clung to the lovely flesh, kissing it quickly, many times, wherever her mouth could find contact. They lay together, side by side. Paula wished furiously that her own body was bare, but she could not release her prize for fear of losing it. When her lips reached Byrne's, they claimed each other long and quietly.

The heaving and pounding in Paula's heart grew calmer. She cradled Byrne's head in her arm and nuzzled the tender earlobes.

"I'll make you happy," Paula promised. "I'll make you forget everything except how good it is to be together."

Byrne spread her fingers up through the back of Paula's head and held it. "You have a lovely dreamland," she murmured. "I envy you."

There was nothing to envy, Paula objected. It was so simple to be together, to crave and satisfy that craving with honest love and eternal devotion. Why must Byrne look troubled when nothing could stop them? Paula kept these thoughts to herself. She did not want to talk, too afraid that Byrne might argue and break the spell of their closeness.

Neither spoke for many moments as they lay together in a still unfulfilled contentment. The incompleteness of their contact fired Paula with tempting promises. She must arrange to stay here a whole night. There wasn't time now to show Byrne all the horizons of her love, but she would, she would. Her mind went to the bed. That ornate bed was so unlike Byrne, so unhappy with its tortured decorations.

"If I ask you something," Paula said, "will you tell me the truth?"

Byrne turned a little and Paula shifted herself above her. She could see the dark pupils, large in the dim light of the room, surrounded by flecks of grey and green and amber.

"Ask anyway," Byrne said. "I'll tell you whatever might concern you."

All of you concerns me, Paula thought. Every move, every breath, every laugh. I want to share your whole life, not peek in at odd moments, know only parts.

"Are there others for you?" Paula said. "I mean right now. Are there?"

Byrne stroked the girl's cheek and ran a finger around the outline of her lips. "You sound like a man," she smiled. "Will you spoil everything so soon?"

Instantly Paula regretted her question. But how could Byrne expect her to love a person only half present, someone almost a ghost? A something that came from nowhere and returned to nowhere?

66

"I'm sorry," she said. "I won't be possessive." Yet she felt possessive and she had every intention of continuing to be possessive. She just wasn't going to let it show. Gradually she would unwind the secret of Byrne without her knowing it. She lay beside the woman, feeling the length of their bodies through her own clothes. Desperately she wanted skin to touch skin. She knew there would be other times, however. It would be best not to rush Byrne. Paula didn't want to frighten her away.

"There are a few things," Byrne offered, "that might be interesting for you to know."

"Like your phone number."

Byrne chuckled. "If you were really smart, you would have noticed it on the phone."

"Well, I'm not smart. But I'm learning."

"The first thing you should learn," Byrne said, pulling herself out from beneath Paula's weight, "is to observe instead of asking questions." She went into the bedroom and Paula followed her.

With disappointment she watched Byrne take trousers out of the closet. She wanted to stop her from getting dressed again. She wanted to pull her down on the bed and possess her completely. If only she knew how! Paula didn't move. Because even more strongly than she felt her desire, Paula wanted Byrne to make some sign that she desired her with equal strength. If Byrne would so much as lift a finger to her, Paula would be her slave. She would stay here and cook and clean and cater to this woman. She would forget Ma and Pa and Mike and live in this fragment of heaven for however long it would last.

Byrne laid her trousers on the bed and took a shirt from a pile in the drawer. She did these things sensibly, as though the moment with Paula had never occurred.

"You came here to sketch. We're not making much progress."

Paula's sight inspected every little object in the room, hoping to learn something new. She saw again the bewitching face of Greta and hated it, knowing instinctively that it had some kind of hold over Byrne.

"I would learn much faster if you would sketch a little, too."

"Me? I could never lift a pencil again. The last piece I did was flung out of a window and it floated away on a merciful breeze."

Paula heard bitterness in the voice. She noticed that Byrne hadn't said that she herself threw it away. Someone else, then? Who? Why? Surely no one could be contemptuous of Byrne's talent.

"You mean it was so important to you that Greta didn't like your work?" Paula's wild thrust hit the mark.

"I hope you never learn," Byrne's voice was hard and remorseless, "about people like Greta."

Paula let Byrne dress, sensing that their mood of pleasure was ended for that evening. They returned to the living room and she resumed her position at the easel. Now, knowing they were not forbidden to her, she could draw portions of Byrne's body without flinching. She wanted to meet Greta. She wanted to come face to face with the poison in Byrne's life and draw it out. If they loved each other, why did Byrne carry the memory so heavily in her heart? Questions pumped into Paula's brain but she knew better than to voice them.

And a plan was beginning to form. She must be very careful not to let Byrne recognize what she was up to. The steps of it were not exactly clear to her yet, but determination would guide her. Byrne must paint again. If she could paint once more and be recognized, then she would realize that life was not ruined for her.

Paula observed her own work. There was talent in it but nothing to rave about. Yes, she would continue to draw and work hard. That would be the bait to lure Byrne back once more to her own creativity and this would conquer Greta's destruction. Paula would win Byrne all to herself. They would be together forever.

She drew until ten-thirty, then sat beside Byrne while she corrected the perspective. Occasionally, Paula pretended not to understand something, forcing Byrne to do a little sketch to explain. Each time Byrne drew an arm or a shoulder slope, Paula congratulated herself.

At eleven o'clock, Byrne said it was time for Paula to leave. The thought of going home, of not seeing Byrne for a whole day made impatience arrive immediately. She wished Byrne would say to come again tomorrow so that she would not feel that she was forcing herself on the woman.

They kissed a gentle good night. The gentleness whirled away into passion and Paula could not release Byrne from her arms. "Let me stay with you," she blurted. "Just tonight."

Byrne tried to disentangle herself. "I'm sorry," she said with reluctance. "Maybe sometime, but not this evening."

So she wasn't going to be alone, Paula realized.

Byrne glanced impatiently at her watch, kissed Paula quickly and closed the door between them.

Lingering in the hallway, Paula straightened her hair. Someone would be coming to Byrne this night. Her body tensed with anger and fearful intuition.

She would wait and discover for herself the person who could make Byrne so restless and even afraid.

5

Paula looked around to see if she could hide behind the staircase and watch from there. The idea of sneaking around like some sort of spy disgusted her. She turned up her coat collar and went outside. Better to stroll along the block or stand across the street. The sky, pink with snow, glowed weirdly. It was cold and her feet made crunching sounds on the frozen sidewalk. The yellow cones from street lamps floated light into the loneliness, setting a stage waiting for the players.

Hands clenched in either pocket, Paula felt the

warmth of her palms beginning to ebb. She climbed the steps of the house directly across the street from Byrne's. From there she could see inside her window. Curtains hindered her view a little but the light behind them aided her. She watched Byrne go to the easel and take away the pad. She saw her bend where the couch would be and guessed that Byrne was gathering her clothes together. Paula smiled with satisfaction. At least Byrne didn't want the other person to know about her. I mean something to her, she thought happily. Maybe just a little, but at least I exist.

Her smile dissolved into curiosity as the sauntering figure of a lone man came into focus. He was short, and obviously unconcerned with the cold because his coat flapped open. When he passed through an arc of light, Paula caught her breath. She must be mistaken. She rushed diagonally across the street to get a better look. She passed close by the figure, almost bumping into it, and she was sure. This was no man.

Wisps of white hair, soft as clouds, fell onto the forehead, not flowing to the shoulders as in the picture, but brutally short. The once delicate features were flabby, swollen with age and degeneration. Those wicked eyes were sunk into folds of black, wrinkled lids. The chin line dissolved in puffs of fat. Only the lips, the sensitive rosy lips, remained in morbid epitaph to the former enchantment.

Paula continued a few steps beyond. Then she turned to watch. The small feet, unprotected by boots, strolled on, moving in a lackadaisical world. She saw her climb Byrne's stairs and push the door open with her shoulder.

Paula retraced her steps and once more climbed the stairs across the street. As if watching a silent film, she watched Greta enter the apartment. Hardly bothering to greet Byrne, she disappeared in the direction of the bedroom. All too soon, Byrne flicked out the lights and left Paula staring into darkness and the black depths of her own imagination.

Paula hardly knew what hour of the night it was when she climbed the last flight and slowly turned the doorknob. Instead of darkness and snoring, she was met by glaring light and silence. Mike had come home. He stood leaning with his arms on the refrigerator, staring greyly at the wall. Her mother sat, wearing the old flowered nightgown. Her braids, disheveled from sleep, fell unnoticed down her back. Phil sat beside her, silently holding her hands.

Paula's first thought was that she was the cause of their anxiety. Then she saw the light in her parents' bedroom. She went to it, and stared at the empty bed.

Slowly, as realization engulfed her, she backed away. Mutely, she questioned them one by one. Where's Pa? But they ignored her.

Oddly, Mike was the first to talk. "The ambulance came hours ago. Where in the hell were you?"

She started to speak but the words choked in her throat. What possible excuse could she give?

"Is he . . . ?" she stuttered.

"We don't know," Phil said. His voice, full of sympathy, did not accuse her.

"Then why is everybody here? Shouldn't someone be at the hospital?"

Mike said, "You're the big help around here. Why don't you go?"

Phil looked at him reproachfully. He continued to interlock fingers with her mother as though infusing her with his own life and strength. He said, "The doctor gave your mother something to calm her down. They wouldn't let Mike go along."

If she ever felt like a deserter, it was now. "Maybe I'd better go there," she said, her voice trembling with guilt.

"What for?" Mike's voice stabbed.

True enough, she thought. What for? What could she do except pace the halls in complete helplessness. She might just as well remain here, in this despairing and frightened place. She felt a tempting urge to join them in their hopelessness but the thought of giving up angered her. Pa wasn't dead yet! For all they knew, he might still outlive them all. But in her heart, she recognized the lie.

If only Ma would say something. Give her some look or a sign that it was not her fault. It wasn't her fault. Even if she had been home, Pa would still be in the hospital. I've got to live my own life, she thought, strangling in the silent gloom and accusation. They can't trap me like an animal. I won't let them!

Resentfully Paula pulled off her clothes and hung them in the closet. The alarm clock said two-fifteen. Automatically she wound it and pulled out the stem.

Phil had to be up at six and here he sat like part of the family, sharing its grief like an actual son-in-law.

Paula wanted to hate him for being a phony but the attention he paid her mother was obviously sincerely felt. He had no thought at this moment for swaying Paula. All he wanted, she could see, was to lend any support he could. His dark face, soft with tenderness, held whatever hope was still possible. Paula couldn't look at him without despising herself.

She stayed in her bedroom, isolated from the mute depression, yet absorbing it passively, like an illness.

If Pa dies, Mike will never forgive me, she thought.

Her self respect weakened and fell away. She heard her mother sigh a long quivering wave of breath. Paula shivered, realizing that her mother had become like a child who must be fondled and cared for. And it was her responsibility, nor Phil's, to hold Ma's hand, yet somehow she couldn't bring herself to go in and replace him. She wasn't even sure that her mother wanted her to.

Oh, I won't stand for it, she fought with herself. I'll move out and mail home my paycheck every week.

The idea mocked her. If she lived away from home there wouldn't be a paycheck to send. Rent and food would consume it.

But suppose she lived with Byrne?

Sure, being a charity case would be just the thing to enchant Byrne. Unwanted, caught between Byrne and Greta, there she would be.

There was nothing she could do. Except marry Phil, of course. Her mind stopped right there. It refused to continue with thoughts of self-sacrifice.

75

Pride rose vaguely, without words, and she knew instinctively that she would not give up for anything. The family would straighten out by itself and she would win Byrne because Byrne was her need. There was no sense in chopping herself into little pieces with remorse.

She heard Mike turn on the faucet and fill a pan with water. "Want some coffee?" he called in to her. He sounded as though he were spitting.

"Yes," she flung back in the same tone and went into the kitchen.

Mike was making an effort to be realistic and sensible. She could see the way he glanced furtively at Phil for approval. Phil winked at him as though they shared a secret together.

Clumsily, Mike set out four cups, spoons, napkins, remembering to get the sugar. He made instant coffee and drank his own black.

Her mother, who seemed suspended between life and death, finally permitted Paula to lead her to the bedroom. She lay down meekly but didn't close her eyes when Paula put out the light.

Just the same, she was glad to get her mother out of the way. The poor woman would need whatever energy she could muster for the days to come, which, Paula knew, would be harder still.

Phil said, "Don't worry about her. The shock will pass. She'll be as good as new by breakfast."

Paula didn't believe him but there was no need to contradict his efforts to comfort her. She felt ill at ease because he didn't seem to notice that she was still the desirable Paula. She could be Mike's twin brother, the way Phil acted. She felt as though she had shed her old skin and become a different person.

Yet she was Paula. All the way through, Paula. The only difference was her new love for Byrne. She's your aunt, Paula thought. If you didn't introduce me to her this would never have happened.

Instantly she wondered how much Phil really knew about Byrne. She felt an impulse to ask him a very cautious question in the hope of discovering something that might make her own way to Byrne easier. Then she remembered what Byrne had said: A smart girl doesn't ask; she observes.

Out of friendliness — Phil was a friend, if nothing else — she said, "How is the paint store coming?"

"Swell," he answered without enthusiasm. "I'll be signing the papers Friday. Already gave my boss two weeks notice."

"I'm glad for you," she replied. And she was glad. Phil was getting ahead. Someday he would forget her and marry a sweet thing who could love him as much as she loved Byrne.

Proudly Mike said, "Phil got me a job with him."

"Well, that's great." Paula acted as if she was surprised so that Mike could lord it over her for a few minutes.

She took Phil's arm and squeezed it with appreciation. Mike needed somebody to look up to and emulate. Paula was thankful that it was Phil. For a second she wished she could be part of all this. The family circle had a solidity and security which she knew there could never be with Byrne. Well, you sacrifice some things to get others, she thought. Love was more important than security.

Mike walked Phil to the door. She stayed behind so that they could have a few private words together.

After Mike locked the door, he came back and cleared the dishes off the table. He looked at Paula with an attempt at pity but it came out as resentment.

"I guess you're pretty tired," he finally said. "Why don't you take the day off tomorrow?"

Her voice choked on the words she wanted to say. There was no way to make Mike know that she loved him; that she needed him as a staunch brother to back her up and help her find strength.

Behind Paula's brave front lay a vast world in which she wandered alone and lost.

When the alarm went off the next morning, Paula turned dizzily in her sleep and reached out a hand to shut it off. Her head ached with fatigue as she squinted into the growing daylight. The events of last night returned to her with the unreality of a nightmare. Her job was a new one. If she stayed home today, they would dock her. She couldn't afford to stay home. Yet she couldn't drag herself up and around to get dressed. If she never had to go to work again, that would be perfectly all right. Those meaningless letters, those impatient voices calling for Mr. This-one and Mr. That-one. She had always accepted work as just a means of survival. Today it seemed unbearable. She fell back to the pillow and decided to stay home.

Within the hour, Paula summoned enough courage to phone the hospital. Even though they couldn't assure her that her father was improving, they told her that things had not turned for the worse. The immediate burden lessened somewhat, her thoughts returned to the strange woman she had seen enter Byrne's apartment.

She listened to see if either her mother or Mike were awake. Deciding it was safe to risk the call, she dialed Byrne's number, then she hung up before the phone started to ring. Too early, of course. She didn't dare appear so anxious. Or stupid. Greta would certainly still be there and want to know what this call was about. She had better not irritate Byrne by rousing Greta's curiosity.

Paula realized that she was thinking more clearly than she had for a very long time. Before Byrne, she had had no reason to. With Phil it had always been a simple matter of emotion expressed when felt. With Byrne there was all the excitement of a game of Russian roulette. One wrong move and she could kill her chances.

Bravely, Mike got up to go to school, the color in his face drained from lack of sleep.

Paula said, "Maybe you ought to stay home today, too."

He snorted at her on his way into the bathroom. She was glad that Mike was acting like a man. She felt proud and good that all Ma's and Pa's struggling had produced a good son, after all.

She put up some cereal for his breakfast, happy to see him eat and pack off for school determined to hide the fears and uncertainties that shook him.

After her mother awoke, Paula dusted the house, washed the dishes and decided to phone Byrne from an outside booth. It would be all right to leave her mother alone for five minutes. By tonight, Mike would be home and she could go out if Byrne would let her. She suddenly wondered if Byrne held an outside job that would keep her away. The idea of a whole day without speaking to her was unendurable.

With relief she heard the receiver lift and Byrne's voice answer, heavy with sleep. Almost noon and she had just gotten out of bed. Pangs of jealousy bit into Paula as she imagined Greta lying beside her all those hours. Yet she kept her voice pleasant.

"I'm sorry to disturb you," she said innocently. "I left my purse in the living room."

Oh yes, Byrne was quite aware that she had left it behind. How come she hadn't returned for it? Bluntly, Paula told her that she knew Byrne was expecting a visitor and she didn't think it wise to barge in.

"I haven't decided," Byrne said, "whether you're shrewd or naive." Her voice sounded pleased and that was all Paula cared about.

When the dime dropped, signaling almost the end of five minutes, Byrne inquired if she was at work.

Paula said no, and waited breathlessly. The magic words came. "If you're free, why don't you stop by for awhile?"

She couldn't refuse. Paula almost ran to hail a cab and have Byrne pay for it when she arrived. She made herself go back upstairs and check on her mother.

The woman had pulled herself together somewhat and was sewing a button on a pair of her father's pants. Paula looked for her mother's breakfast dishes but found none. With her coat still on, Paula warmed up what was left of the oatmeal and made coffee.

Ma ate while Paula told her that she had called the hospital and Pa was doing fine.

No ray of light crept into her mother's eyes. Nor

80

did Paula's tone hold true conviction. She phoned the hospital again. Still the nurse put her off with the same reply that held so little hope.

Paula knew that if she sat around the house all day she would go crazy. Even if not to see Byrne, she would have to go somewhere. What kind of company could she be for her mother, when she herself was so distraught? Might just as well get away and leave her in peace.

She had started for the door when her mother's voice called her back, sounding brittle and unfamiliar, as if all the juice of life had been wrung from her.

"Where are you going?"

The question caught Paula off guard. This was a strange time for her mother to care about her doings.

"Out for a while." It wasn't a lie, yet it sounded like one.

"Where do you go when you say you're going out?" The hollow voice seemed to be coming from a great distance. It frightened Paula and upset her.

"What difference does it make?" She wanted to avoid the question. "I was too tired to go to work."

"I want you to tell me where you're going, Paula." She stirred the coffee aimlessly, but her manner was oddly persistent.

Paula remained in the hallway. She didn't want to come back. This was wasting her time, the precious minutes that could be spent with Byrne. Even so, she couldn't take advantage of her mother. Not now, she just couldn't.

"If you must know, I'm going to visit a friend."

"Which friend? Who is home in the middle of the day?"

"Lots of people." She couldn't evade the question

forever. Either she would have to lie or walk out without answering.

Paula took a few steps back toward the kitchen. Heavy steps, regretting each one. "Look, Ma, if you want me to stay home with you, just say so. I don't think it's fair to give me a third degree when we're both so upset."

"You're not acting like my daughter." Her voice was flat, expressionless. "You've turned into a stranger lately. I still have the right to know who's influencing you."

Oh, Lord, it was going to drag on all afternoon. The remnants of her patience fluttered on the tip of Paula's tongue. "I'm upset because of Pa," she said. "The way you are, too. Think you've been acting like yourself? When did you ever sit at the table like that?"

Her mother gazed at her steadily. Paula's words didn't fool her. "All right. If you're getting into trouble, nobody will help you but yourself."

Paula relaxed and kissed her mother on the forehead. "I'm too big to get into trouble," she said.

"Yes."

Quickly she left before her mother could find other threads of Paula's life to unravel. She cursed herself for forgetting to take carfare. Then, with a burst of self-assurance, she hailed a cab.

The driver pulled up in front of the brownstone and Paula told him to wait. She ran inside and explained to Byrne. Byrne pulled some bills from her own purse and gave them to Paula. Absorbed with these trifles, Paula did not notice, at first, the marks on Byrne's arms. She came back in and bounced onto the couch, throwing her head back, smiling up at the ceiling. The unaccustomed feeling of not being at the office flapped gleefully inside her like a young bird trying its wings.

Byrne said, "I was just about to make some breakfast."

"Oh, let me make it," Paula said, leaping up and dashing after Byrne to the kitchen area. It was not the old fashioned sort of kitchen, but an alcove off the living room. A circular booth of black leather substituted for a regular dining table.

They both reached for the refrigerator door at the same time. It was then that Paula noticed the red streaks swollen on Byrne's arm. She was about to exclaim over them, but the look in Byrne's eyes stilled her. It wasn't a challenging glance or expression that dared Paula to pry. Rather, there was something that beseeched Paula to leave her in peace. The bantering laughter had vanished.

Paula struggled with her concern. Her natural desire to exclaim over the ugly bruises fought against her intelligence which cautioned silence. Instead of questioning Byrne, she reached for the bacon. While she lay strips of meat into the frying pan, her gaze firmly held to the task, Byrne broke eggs and stirred them. Paula thought, if she respects me, she'll give me some explanation. At the same time, she wasn't sure if she deserved yet this right to Byrne's respect.

Paula concentrated on breakfast, glad for the excuse of eating to avoid meaningless conversation.

By the time they wandered into the living room with their coffee cups, Paula had recovered from her awkwardness. Immediately she went to the easel. Her sketch pads were nowhere to be seen. She remembered that Byrne had put them away the night before . . . after she left.

Byrne said, "Oh, I stashed them back in the closet. I didn't suppose we would be having another lesson again, quite so soon." Her voice was dry, but it held a hint of gladness.

"If it bores you . . ." Paula began.

"Quite the contrary. I enjoy you and your enthusiasm. It's good for me, you know. You help me forget things for a while." She turned for the bedroom. Paula stayed her with a hand on the bruised arm.

"Don't bother," she said. "I'll get them." She was glad for a reason to go back into that bedroom. It held the clues that she must discover. If only she could be smart enough to piece them together.

Byrne let her go. Paula went eagerly, but with some distaste. The bedroom was like a dead thing from which she must not avert her eyes. Courage and hope came to Paula's aid because she knew that Byrne was giving her the chance to discover whatever she could.

Standing in the doorway, Paula stared about this room of hidden tortures. The sheets, tangled with blankets, lay in a heap. One pillow dangled halfway to the floor. The other seemed dashed against the headboard, its striped ticking hanging out like ripped guts. Violence was everywhere. The cigarette case gaped open on its side. A comb had landed on the windowsill. Beneath it on the floor lay one curtain that had been torn from its rod.

Steadily Paula observed these signs of rage. One

question, more demanding than all the others: Did Greta do this? It must be Greta. Surely Byrne would not inflict those marks upon herself. She righted the cigarette box and searched the angelic face of evil. She recalled the degraded, puffy creature who had passed beneath the street lights. Certainly Greta was capable of anything. It occurred to Paula that this woman was not in her right mind. Oh, my poor Byrne, she thought, why do you feel responsible for this creature? For she knew Byrne was strong enough to free herself, if only she wanted to do so.

Miserably, Paula went to the closet. She put her cheek against Byrne's jacket and clung to it, begging knowledge and understanding. The intimate smell of Byrne's clothes flamed her agony into tears. Goodness, warmth, love was Byrne. Not insane fury that shredded life's meaning into tatters. She swallowed her tears and reached up for the sketch pads neatly stacked on the shelf. As she pulled them down, a shower of loose drawings fluttered and scattered about her shoulders. Carefully, she retrieved them. As she sorted the portraits, their serenity and blending colors made her calmer. For each was signed with the initials B.E.

When she had put them back, she left the room and went, businesslike, to the easel. Byrne lay on the couch, her coffee cup resting on her trousers buckle.

"No comment?" Byrne said, her eyes narrowing alertly as Paula flipped open to a clean page.

"No comment." Paula's voice was steady. She wet her lips and quickly began to draw. She would show Byrne how well she could take all this. Paula's importance, after all, was making Byrne forget. Her purpose would be to make her forget, not for a while, but forever. She concentrated on the reclining figure to draw its magnificent lines and shadows.

When she had been sketching for a while and Byrne seemed relaxed, Paula said casually, "It would be nice if you'd tell me your last name. You know, just for the record." She kept her gaze on the picture so Byrne could not tell if Paula was leading up to anything.

"You're a funny girl," Byrne said, and Paula knew she had made the right move. "The reason I like you is not because you're talented. God knows, talented people are a dime a dozen. You have courage also, and faith in something that seems to promise nothing but unhappiness. I admire you for it."

Paula thought, I have faith in you, Byrne. She kept her silence. Better to let Byrne talk, if she would. Paula continued drawing.

"Yes, I like you very much." Byrne's voice was low and flowed gently. Paula sensed the door to Byrne beginning to open. "You're emotional, yet you know how to control it. People much older than yourself rarely learn that. You're wise with nature's wisdom."

Paula caught a quick glance of daylight quietly playing among the strands of red gold in Byrne's hair. Speak, my darling, speak. Share the secrets with me that are tearing you.

As though she heard her thoughts, Byrne continued. "If you were anyone else, Paula, I would send you away. In fact I don't even know, now, whether I shouldn't. Perhaps I don't because I am selfish. You offer . . ."

A jiggling of the doorknob halted Byrne's words.

They both turned to it. The knob rattled, waited a few moments, rattled harder.

"Damn it to hell!" Byrne's voice rasped.

Fists pounded on the other side.

Paula said nothing. She stood still. She watched Byrne.

Knuckles drummed insistently, demanding attention.

Byrne flung herself off the couch. She strode to the door. Paula held her breath as Byrne opened it.

Head tilted like a puppy's, Greta looked up at Byrne.

"I think I want to go to the movies." Her voice floated like wind high above trees. "Is it all right if I go to the movies, dear? You won't be angry?" Aimlessly, her fingers moved in the air. Dainty fingers with jagged skin stained iodine brown.

"Of course I won't be angry."

Paula listened with astonishment to the soothing tone Byrne used, as though speaking to a baby.

"You go to the movies and have a good time. Have you enough money?"

"I have a dollar left from what you gave me. It only costs sixty-five cents."

Byrne's hand went to her pocket.

"No, don't give me any more. I might lose it." The face puckered its lips. Byrne leaned over and kissed them. Greta made a happy childlike sound. Then she turned and strolled away.

Byrne closed the door and leaned heavily against it. She took a cigarette and lit it slowly. Paula saw anger working itself outward, stiffly into the lips, flaming bright in the slanting eyes. "So that's it,"

Byrne said. She clutched one hand around the matchbook. Knuckled bulged whitely. Her anger didn't stab at Paula, it curled around herself and choked her blood into red spots on her cheeks. "That's Greta, my dear. Or what's left of her." She came across the room and stood very close to Paula. She stared full into the girl's face but did not focus on her. It unnerved Paula to be looked at so hard and yet not seen. "You were jealous of competition. A healthy young thing like you was jealous of that."

Paula struggled to make some sound, to make Byrne feel her presence. "Yes, I was jealous," she hit back. "And I'm still jealous of the past I can't fight. It's not fair for something like Greta to be my competition." She jabbed her pencil at the paper and ripped a dark line furiously down the page. "How can I fight a nightmare? Why must you live with it? Drag everything that's good in you down into a senseless misery?"

"Why, indeed," Byrne echoed. "It's so simple for you to make up rules on how to live and be happy. I should chuck Greta into a sanitarium and forget she ever existed. Forget those years we innocently lived together. Wouldn't it be convenient for you if I could say it wasn't my fault, my cowardice that sent Greta away."

"Whatever you did," Paula urged softly, "was not cowardly."

Byrne snorted and turned over a new page of Paula's book. "Let's drop it," she said. "I haven't the stomach."

Paula flung the pencil aside and pulled Byrne down with her to the couch. "I don't care what you did. You aren't responsible for Greta's mind." She put her arms around Byrne's waist and pressed her cheek to her chest. "But you are responsible for mine because you're torturing me. I act like a big shot. I don't know what I'm doing, really. Last night if you had let me, I wouldn't even have known . . ." her voice trailed away.

"You're smarter than you realize," Byrne muttered. She put her lips to the girl's hair and Paula felt the warm breath on her scalp.

"If I were smart, I would have you all to myself with nothing to stop us from being happy." The closeness of Byrne weakened her. She craved the lips and the flesh of her body. Good sense disappeared. She buried her mouth in the woman's neck.

"If you stay with me, you will never know any happiness." Byrne's tone was bitter with self-hatred.

"I love you. You can't stop me from loving you." She clung to Byrne and moved her head down to where her shirt opened.

"No, I can't stop you," Byrne whispered, her voice vibrant with growing passion. "But I can destroy you."

Paula laughed into the warm flesh. "I'm not Greta," she murmured, "so you can't. I'm Paula."

"Yes. Paula," Byrne said curiously, as though aware for the first time of this new person in her arms.

Paula was not content to remain like this, with contact between them only half complete. She wanted Byrne to take her into the bedroom. Yet how could they go in there? The remains, the echoes of Greta, would mock them.

If only we could leave this place, Paula thought. Go far, far away where no past could interfere. If only for a weekend she could have Byrne all to herself.

"Paula," Byrne said. "I want you to do something for me."

"Anything. You know that."

"Then listen carefully and don't question what I say." She held the girl tightly and Paula felt the buckle pressing against her own stomach. "I want you to go. There is nothing here, with me, that can be any good for you. Even if you don't believe me now, in time you will see the truth of it."

She hugged Byrne with all her strength. A frightened, sick feeling swam through her. Leave Byrne! When at last she had found the one thing in life worth fighting for?

"Don't struggle against me, Paula. Just do as I say. Trust it blindly, for my sake, no matter how much it hurts."

Wordlessly Paula shook her head. She couldn't speak. Her throat tightened with desperation. Give Byrne up? Nothing short of death could make her do that. Not even Byrne herself. She had to show Byrne that Greta couldn't stop her. She realized that if Byrne did not care for her, she wouldn't be asking this. She would enjoy their moments, indifferent to what finally happened. As long as Byrne cared, Paula would not leave her.

Somehow, Paula freed herself from Byrne's arms. She stood up, swaying from her own confusion. There must be something she could do to prove to Byrne how wrong it was for her to ask this.

Byrne, mistaking Paula's action, said, "That's a smart girl. Cut yourself off clean and sharp. The wound will heal quicker that way."

Paula hardly heard her. Engrossed in her confused thoughts, she stumbled through a jungle of words, trying to find the right ones.

"I'm not leaving you, Byrne." Unable to look at the woman, she lifted her gaze to the beautiful portrait. "Don't ask me to do something I'll regret for the rest of my life." Her voice was hardly more than a whisper. "Long ago, you listened to reason. You were sensible and did what was supposed to be the right thing. But it was all wrong for you. It would be just as wrong for me to leave you now."

Byrne said nothing. Paula didn't know how she was taking it. She couldn't face Byrne, knowing that her words must be cutting into her. "You don't save me by asking me to go," Paula continued. "If you care for me the smallest bit, you'll let me stay with you. Maybe I'm a bigger coward than you realize. I haven't the will to go out into that lonely world again since I've found you. If you've learned anything from leaving Greta, you must know how I can't bear to sacrifice this wonderful thing you've given me." She sighed wearily.

"If you don't go," Byrne answered, "I won't be responsible for you." The words were precise, yet underlying them was a hint of gratefulness. For the first time since she had met Byrne, Paula was convinced that she was in some way needed. A strange peace floated around her. And she was ready for whatever destiny might have in store.

She turned and gazed at Byrne from a distance. Their glances met and each was touched by the other's smile. Byrne got up and went to the window. She pulled down the shade. A semi-darkness covered the room. Paula stood where she was until Byrne approached her. She let the woman draw her into the circle of her embrace. The full, sincere kiss told Paula she had won. And slowly, with the sure instinct of love, Byrne drew Paula to the couch and taught her the way of fulfillment.

6

Afterward, Paula saw and heard a change come over Byrne. The crust of challenge that coated Byrne's words broke and fell away. What had been the cold beauty of her form seemed tinged with a golden warmth. And Paula, soothed by the experience of completion, floated gently into sleep, secure within this new intimacy.

When she awoke, the room had darkened with the overtones of night. She yawned and sought Byrne's cheek with her lips. Byrne held the girl's head against her shoulder. She herself lay with her eyes closed and Paula did not want to break this lingering peace. If only they could stay thus forever.

"It's getting late," Byrne said, stretching into a more comfortable position. There wasn't much room on the couch but their passion had made it adequate.

"Is it?" Paula said, not caring. She stroked the line of Byrne's ribs with the tip of a forefinger.

"Perhaps you'd better go."

"Do you want me to?"

Byrne shook her head, an easy grin lifting the curve of her lips.

"Then I won't," Paula said and nuzzled her face deeper into the line of Byrne's throat. The delicious sweetness of Byrne's skin mingled with the dampness of sleep.

"Yes, you will," Byrne insisted, the words exhaled against Paula's forehead. "But you'll come back tomorrow."

". . . and tomorrow and tomorrow and tomorrow . . ." Paula echoed.

"As long as it lasts."

Confidently Paula shifted herself and sat up.

Tomorrow would be always.

She dressed, already feeling the loneliness of parting. "It will be hard to sleep by myself," she said. "I'll never be able to again."

"Perhaps sometime you can stay."

All the way home, Paula dreamed of spending a night with Byrne beside her. She dreaded the empty bed. Night seemed friendless, a stranger intruding between herself and love.

Slowly, she climbed the flights of the dingy house. This place where she had lived most of her life had become a thing unreal, a theatre in which she would have to act until tomorrow.

She turned the doorknob but it did not yield. She pushed. The door remained closed. An unaccustomed silence hung behind it. She paused and listened. No voices, no sound of movement could she hear. Quickly, Paula found her key and let herself in.

"Ma?" she called. "Mike?"

No one. The emptiness threatened her. She went from room to room uneasily. All were empty.

She sat down in her coat and tried to collect her thoughts. Tensely she went to the phone and dialed the hospital.

When she had hung up, she wiped the sweat from her palms and raced out again to join her family.

In the hospital, the noise of her shoes along the white corridor resounded loudly. Nurses passing by hardly noticed her. When she joined the huddled group, she couldn't speak to them.

Ma glanced at her but didn't nod hello. The cold set of her features brought sharp angles to her nose and cheekbones. The usually black shining hair was dull and uncombed. Mike sat bent over, staring down at the smooth floor between his knees, his hands clasped tightly together. Paula felt as if she had been away from them for fifty years.

Only Phil recognized her presence. She looked at him, pleading for some news. He led her a little way down the hall and leaned her against the wall.

"I'm afraid this is it," he whispered. His dark eyes, bright with compassion and sorrow spoke more than the words. Paula suddenly realized that Phil felt this as strongly as she should have been feeling it.

"Is he . . ." She could not finish the sentence.

"No. But if he gets through the night, it'll be some kind of miracle." He watched her, Paula knew, wishing that she would, in some way, lean against him for strength. She wanted to give herself up to him. She wanted to let him support the heaviness of guilt dragging at her shoulders, aching in all her limbs. But she was not Phil's, could not seek him for comfort. She turned away and joined Mike's vigil on the bench.

The surgical odor crept into her clothes. Though the place was warm, she did not think of taking off her coat. How long could they sit, waiting like slaves for the white-robed king to come out from behind those doors and tell them that it was all over? She wondered if her father was aware. Did he lie in some steel bed feeling the slow ebb and loss of life, never to return? Sometimes people went on like this for days. Would the end come for him mercifully soon?

Oh Byrne, Byrne! Don't waste the precious moments on a past that can never be repaired. Live with me now, while we can still feel it.

Mike stirred. Paula looked at his face. The rims of his eyes were red and swollen. He must be thinking of all his small, selfish acts, cursing himself with regret. She wanted to tell him there was no point in doing that. You have to look forward, always. The words sounded corny, even in her thoughts. She sighed, yearning to join her mother.

The old woman was turned with her back halfway to Paula. Her shoulders slumped beneath the worn material of her coat. Ma hadn't lived either. The priceless years had slipped by her in drudgery. What

96

happiness had she known, raising two ungrateful brats who would only leave her in the end?

I'm going to live, Paula thought with sudden intensity. I won't sit here and flay myself with remorse. If I don't make my own happiness, no one will do it for me.

She looked at Phil who stood alone against the wall. If she had married him, there would be kids just like herself and Mike. The rat race of growing up, giving birth, dying. Life could give so much more than this. She wished she could tell Phil. But he, too, was part of the rat race. She felt sorry for him.

Mike's head lifted as a door opened. The doctor came out, his forehead wrinkled into what was supposed to pass for sympathy. How many times a day did he see death? Telling the family was just one more part of his daily routine. Paula stood up. He smiled, patted her shoulder and steered her over to Ma.

"You might as well go home and get some rest," he said. His tone surprised Paula. It was full of sincere regret. "He went easily in his sleep, Mrs. Temple. At least we can be thankful for that."

Ma looked at him mutely. Tears welled and ran swiftly in two single streams down her cheeks. Her face didn't rumple up. She just looked quietly and the tears were all that moved.

Paula fell to her knees and put her face in her mother's lap. She encircled the plump waist with both arms. Her mother's hands did not move to touch her. They remained grimly and unbendingly at either side of her body.

When Paula realized this, she moved away to let

Mike take her place. She stood off to one side and watched Mike bravely put an arm around Ma's shoulder. He would take her home, Paula knew. Mike had suddenly become big enough, and responsible. She let Phil walk with her to the elevator, glad that he had taught Mike something of maturity.

They stepped out of the building whipped by the fierce wind from the East River. She let it fly at her coat, slapping the hem open against her leg. Nothing could reach through the numbness surrounding her. A huge gap had come into the world.

Phil didn't try to make conversation. He simply walked beside her, leaving her to the agony of her own thoughts. She wondered bitterly why he hadn't stayed behind to walk with her mother.

When they reached the avenue, he said, "Come on, I'll get you some coffee." He did not try to make her feel ashamed. Simple friendliness and a desire to keep her company at this sad time, motivated him.

She let him take her into a small restaurant. He found them a table in a corner and held the chair out while she sat down.

He ordered black coffee for them both and two pieces of pastry.

"Mike's a good kid," he said, just to be talking. He sensed the need of words now to tie her to reality. "Temperamental like you, sort of, but a good kid."

She felt herself floating away, like a kite suddenly cut loose. Staring at Phil across the table, his dark cheeks suffused with color from the night cold, she remembered that this was Manhattan, First Avenue, and the days would go on for her despite everything.

She said, "Yes, Mike's fine. He can take care of Ma, now."

"And do a good job, too."

I'm not needed, she thought. And not wanted.

"He starts at the store same day I do. He'll be earning enough to fill in for —"

"Pa," Paula finished.

She looked at the crisp pastry with white triangles of cheese showing at each end.

"Go on, try a piece," Phil urged, not picking up his own.

She lifted half but it tasted like nothing. Like cotton in her mouth. She put it down again and played with the handle of the coffee cup. Someone dropped a coin into the juke box. Rock and roll blared.

Phil motioned to the counterman to turn the volume down.

The music settled into subdued chords.

"Maybe I don't owe you anything," Paula said. Her lips moved mechanically as though something had wound her up. "But I want you to know how much I appreciate that you still treat me like a human being."

"Don't let them get you down."

"I don't mean the family. I mean . . . between us." She had to go on. A need to clear the air between them impelled her with its own energy. "Maybe you think I hate you for what happened between us that night. I don't. Something just changed inside me that I have no control over. Believe me, if I could love any man, it would be you."

"Then there isn't somebody else?" His eyes took on a gleam that she had not seen there since that first day with Byrne.

"Well, there isn't another man," she said.

He put his cup down and leaned across toward her. "All these times you've been going out? It wasn't some other guy?"

"No," she said dully.

"I'll be damned," he said softly.

The splattering of a fresh hamburger newly placed on the grill filled the air with an odor of grease.

"Don't question me," she continued. "Just know that I wasn't stolen out from under your nose by some flashy attraction." Hurriedly she searched through her purse for cigarettes, not wanting to hear his words of gratefulness.

She made him take her home and did not let him pursue the subject. Her duty to Phil was done.

Ma and Mike were already home by the time Phil brought her upstairs. They wandered through the rooms, not talking. Paula hoped that the doctor had given Ma some pills to put her to sleep, but she didn't ask. There was little else Paula could do except undress and go to bed.

She slept fitfully, waking every so often without remembering what it was that caused the burden in her heart. She had to struggle to recall that Pa was gone. She lay awake, listening for sounds. Hearing none, she knew that her mother sat in the bedroom thinking nothing, feeling nothing.

When the light of morning fingered into her room she dressed and put up a pot of water for tea. Tea would be better than coffee if her mother wanted anything. She didn't know what arrangements one made for funerals. The idea of relatives and flowers made her ill. There was no possible excuse to go to Byrne this evening. She could not in clear conscience leave her family now. At ten o'clock she phoned Byrne but there was no answer.

She remembered to call the office and tell them, plugging her ears against the conventional sympathy. She could easily take off a few days and not have to worry about the paycheck.

Though nobody spoke to her, she made meals and pulled the house together. The job of sorting her father's clothes to be given away Ma would have to do. Paula hoped it could be finished with soon.

In the afternoon, she phoned Byrne again. The voice of her beloved gave her reason to go on with this hopeless round of family and activity. She told Byrne very simply what had happened, so that she would not expect Paula to get away that night. She would phone Byrne every day and come as quickly as she could.

Uninvited, Phil came up later that day and took over the making of arrangements. Without protest Paula let him, glad to be rid of this duty. She did not believe in the fuss and bother that was given to a person after death instead of while he was alive. Thank heaven, Pa had enough insurance to cover the costs and take care of Ma well enough, with Mike's salary added now.

Phil wrote out the lists of things that had to be done. Ma and Mike helped him. Every now and then he glanced around for Paula to let her know she wasn't invisible. Silently, Paula thanked him for it.

101

* * * * *

One day it was over, and Paula knew she could resume her own life. The apartment, rearranged, looked less cluttered. Paula dressed and went to work, the way you finally have to do when everything is settled.

At lunchtime she phoned Byrne eagerly to tell her she would be over that evening. It had been only a week, but the yearning in Paula's heart swelled in gigantic need.

She rushed over directly from work, hardly able to stand still until Byrne answered the doorbell.

She swept into Byrne's embrace, eyes closed, lips tingling in a hunger for her kisses. Paula felt Byrne's response, the deep breathing movement of her chest, the pressing of her thighs against her own.

"God, but I missed you," Byrne said, as Paula ran her fingers through her hair.

Paula opened the first button of Byrne's shirt and pressed her face into the space there. The warm flesh swelled on either side of Paula's cheeks and she sighed with desire and happiness.

Byrne kicked the door closed. They settled snugly together on a chair, too intent with each other to require all the space of the couch.

"My darling," Paula murmured, needing no other words beyond these. She kissed the light spray of freckles across Byrne's nose. Kissed the rounded eyelids, feeling the brush of the lashes. Kissed the eyebrows, the forehead, the burnished silken hair. They grinned at each other, hands clasped tightly, legs intertwined.

"All I kept thinking," Byrne said, "was that I'd

have you soon. One more day and I'd have you. Baby . . . baby . . . how can I need you so much?" She held Paula's face and inspected it. "Poor darling. You looked dragged out. I hope it hasn't been too rough for you."

Engulfed by Byrne's presence, Paula could remember nothing. "I'm fine," she said. "We're together and I'm fine."

"If you're ready for it," Byrne said, "I have a surprise for you." She emptied Paula from her lap and, taking her hand, led her into the bedroom.

Paula stared. "Darling, how wonderful!" She sighed, looking at the low modern bed cleanly covered with a nubby, violet spread. The room had a special, brightness that filtered in between the bamboo shades. Only the cigarette case remained to speak of Greta.

"I thought it would be easier this way," Byrne folded the spread back, brought Paula over and put her down on the cool fresh sheets.

How different it all was here, on a bed, together and free. They sprawled and lingered at their ease. Paula abandoned herself to the luxuriant weight of Byrne's body full on her own. The hours fled with no word of Greta or the world to disturb them.

"Someday," Paula said, "perhaps we can live together and share this every night."

"Like a married couple?" Byrne laughed.

"Yes, if you want to call it that. I would love to wake up in the morning and make breakfast for you."

"See me off to work? Have supper ready when I come home at six?"

"You're teasing me."

103

"Not at all. I hadn't realized just how conventional you really are." She rolled with Paula to one side of the bed and nipped her earlobe playfully.

"It's not convention," Paula said, "if I want to do things for you."

"Maybe not. What would you call it?"

"Love."

"I thought you hated the way your folks lived. Isn't that what you told me?"

"This isn't like that," Paula said with distaste. "First of all, you're not poor."

"Phil won't be poor either, in a couple of years."

"Why do you bring him into it?"

"You've mentioned him a number of times yourself, these last few days."

"I'm grateful to Phil." Paula brought the pillow down under her chin and hugged it. "He got me out of the mess. Don't talk about him in the same breath as you talk about us."

"All right, darling. Maybe I'm just wondering if you care for him more than you realize."

"Nonsense! If I could move in with you right now and sign a guarantee to stay here for the next thousand years, nothing would make me happier."

"Well, what's stopping you?" Byrne pulled the pillow away and put her face next to Paula's.

Paula could hardly realize what Byrne had offered. She regarded her seriously, prepared to find the teasing smile. It wasn't there.

"Are you really serious? Are you asking me to move in here with you?"

"This is a new bed, isn't it? No one has ever been on it but you." The green eyes were new as spring.

104

Paula had more sense than to speak of Greta. Undoubtedly she was still around. But perhaps Byrne had a reason now to do something other than submit to her old love — and old guilt. If Paula were with her all the time, maybe Byrne would eventually stop blaming herself for Greta. Paula did not dare miss this opportunity to make Byrne whole, to have her completely to herself.

"You know I want to be with you always. Of course I'll stay with you."

Paula felt herself on the verge of a different life. If gaining Byrne had been the start of a change, living with her would complete it. Byrne had never told her what she did with her days. Whatever it was, Paula wanted to share it. Money, which had always been such an obstacle, seemed unimportant here. Byrne had volunteered to send a check home in Paula's name every week.

"That wouldn't be fair," Paula protested. "I'll keep my job or get another."

"Wouldn't it be more unfair to stay away from me all day long? What's the use of this money if I can't spend it on you?"

Out of habit, Paula continued to object. The thought of living without needing to work was something she couldn't imagine. Everybody worked. People just had to. Only pregnant women didn't.

"Look at it this way," Byrne suggested. "You're merely stopping temporarily. Instead of going to that crumby, meaningless job, you'll stay at home and learn to paint. With a few months' training, depending upon how good you are, you'll be able to find a job in commercial art that'll pay you three times what you're earning now. Doesn't that make more sense than battling that typewriter until you drop over the keys?"

Paula had to admit that Byrne was right. Not only did she have a lover, now, she had a teacher as well, one who would help her better herself in every way. Paula felt like a chosen being. She could hardly say a word because nothing would express what she felt in her heart.

Paula brought in the electric percolator with two cups on a tray and sat down. Filled with her new station in life, she only wanted to be still and silent to relish it. How could all these wonderful things be happening to her, Paula? It was all too good. Something must be wrong somewhere, but she could think of nothing that was not perfect. The miracle of her new existence floated around her. She had to sit and believe it whole; it just didn't make sense, otherwise.

Byrne watched her being consumed by her dreams. Smiling gently, she herself went to fill the percolator because Paula had forgotten.

The girl could only touch the bed and say to herself: Not Byrne's bed. *Our* bed. *Our* cups. *Our* apartment. She lay down then sat up. She understood for the first time what it meant to pinch yourself to see if you were dreaming.

Byrne filled their cups while Paula, finally able to speak, chatted on and on about their plans, both real and fanciful.

"Don't run away with yourself, darling," Byrne advised. "You might find this different from what you imagine."

If she means Greta, Paula thought, that doesn't

worry me. She looked at the cigarette case and wet her lips. There were many secrets between Greta and Byrne that she could never know, which meant that she must be more powerful than both.

They discussed what Paula would say to her family about leaving home. Paula was convinced that her mother didn't give a hoot where she went or what she did. The memory of her mother ignoring her in the hospital burned hotly inside. No mother can treat a daughter like that and not expect her to go away, Paula believed. Her mother actually wanted her to leave. Savage memories of her family, self-torturing thoughts of herself being taken away when the worst was taking place, flooded through her. She stared blankly into a corner of the room, wishing she could cut herself off from family which now seemed the cause only of pain and never hear about those people again.

"Don't be childish," Byrne said. "You've hurt them as much as they've hurt you. Sometime, sweetheart, you'll all get together and forgive each other."

Paula said nothing. She wanted to be free of them until she could think about them — and herself — without this horrible rage and guilt.

If it was up to Paula, she wouldn't have returned home even that night. She made herself dress and was combing her hair when the doorbell rang. They looked at each other. Byrne hastened into slacks and shirt. They both knew it wasn't Greta's ring. Paula stood at the dressing table mirror putting on her lipstick, waiting. She didn't care who was at the door so long as it wasn't Greta, but her hand froze in front of her face as she heard the voice.

"Well, if it isn't my little nephew," Byrne's voice said, brittle, trying to sound amused. "What can I do for you on this cold night?"

7

Paula tiptoed to the bedroom door and shut it gently. She stood pressed against it, listening. Their voices came through to her muffled but easily understood.

"I didn't come for any favors this time," she heard Phil say. "Just a few kind words. Maybe a drink."

"Why do you need kind words? Businessmen need customers, not kind words." The slap of the refrigerator door told Paula that Byrne was getting ice cubes.

"The hell with business," Phil said.

"All right, to hell with it. What then?"

"Listen," Phil paused, probably gulping a swallow. "You're an old hand at certain things. What did you make of that girl I brought with me Sunday?"

Old hand, Paula thought. Did Phil know about his aunt's odd interests?

"You mean Paula?" Byrne said, as if surprised. The tone of her voice revealed how very much in control of herself she was.

"Of course, Paula. Who else was here?" His irritation was not with Byrne. It was an irritation of self that stemmed from doubt and worry. Paula realized she hadn't done a very good job of consoling him that night. If anything, she had probably made matters worse. He might be able to accept the idea of competition with another man. Competing with something unknown must be unbearable.

"I thought her a very fine girl," Byrne said. "Attractive, intelligent. Why?"

"Do you think she liked me?"

Paula heard a long silence in which Byrne might be sipping her own drink, stalling to decide how to put things.

"She seemed fond of you. Of course, you were too concerned with your own purposes to notice that she might have had other thoughts on her mind also."

"I guess you're right," Phil said regretfully. "The truth of the matter is she's given me the gate." Another pause. "I mean it. Left me for no good reason. But there must be a reason, if I weren't too dumb to see it."

"I'm certainly sorry," Byrne said. "What can I do to help?"

110

"She kind of took to this idea of painting."

"And since I do give lessons, you thought that I could get in touch with her. If she visits me a few times, perhaps she'd tell me what's on her mind. Is that what you mean? That's not very fair of you, Phil."

"So what? I want to marry the girl, Byrne. Anything's fair."

"Are you quite sure your feelings aren't sore and sensitive because she's playing hard to get?"

Paula, afraid to move for fear of making a noise, listened intently.

"Sure as anything. I wanted to marry her almost the first time I saw her. She's that kind of person. Only I thought it would be easier on her, on us both if we waited until I could get something better than the two-bit job I had."

Paula heard Byrne put her glass on the bookshelf.

"If it's that important to you, I'll see what I can do with her."

"You're really the greatest." Phil's voice was vibrant. "Here's her phone number."

When the door had closed, Paula waited for Byrne to come tell her it was safe. She waited a few minutes but Byrne didn't approach the bedroom. Finally Paula opened the door gently and peered out.

Byrne was standing in the living room, contemplating her empty glass, swinging the melting ice cube around in slow circles at the bottom.

"So," Paula said, a grin flitting across her lips. "Are you going to phone me?"

"I don't know," Byrne replied, ignoring Paula's attempt at humor. "He's not one you shake off easily. I'm not even sure that you really should."

Paula flopped onto the couch and finished the rest of Phil's drink. "Are we going to go through that again? I like him very much. He's the dearest, sweetest thing in the world. But I don't love him." Paula's voice was rising. "Byrne, I don't love him!"

"Stop shouting."

"Stop picking on me. Can't you understand that I love you, Byrne? He didn't do a thing for me when we tried it out. What better proof can you want?"

Byrne took the glass away from Paula and set both their glasses on the table. "Snap judgments don't mean anything. For some people it takes a lot of practice to get used to a man."

"Oh, you're impossible!" Paula folded her arms and pouted with aggravation.

"All right, we'll drop it."

When Byrne relented, Paula became sorry that she had been so harsh. She held her arms out to Byrne and brought her down beside her on the couch. "Now, you make sure to phone me tomorrow evening. That'll give me a good excuse to pack. Imagine, I'll be moving in with Phil's approval." She laughed and patted Byrne's cheek. "Don't forget that no matter how childish I am, I love you."

She rode home feeling very sorry for Phil. There was no doubt in her mind how much he cared for her but he should find a girl suited to him, good enough for him. That girl could never be herself. Even if she left Byrne, she couldn't go to Phil. There would always be the comparison between his blunt, harsh way of doing things and Byrne's graceful, almost catlike movement and attraction. She wondered if any man could ever interest her again.

Paula realized with a slight shock that she had

become what people called "queer." How strange yet the strange thing was not the finding of what she was; it was the discovery that this knowledge of herself did not feel queer at all. To Paula, it seemed truly the most natural thing in the world.

When she got out of the cab, she started up the steps and then stopped midway to the first landing. She didn't want to go in. Not just yet. It wasn't early but anything she could do to delay coming into the strained and tense atmosphere of that apartment would be welcome. She turned around and descended the steps. Without thinking, she crossed the street and entered a bar.

The heavy odor of beer assailed her nostrils. Four men played table bowling. A frowzy old woman sat in the far corner staring up at the fights on television. Paula found a stool at the bar, and climbed on. Uncomfortable, she was sorry she had come in but did not want to leave now that she was here.

She ordered scotch and water because that was what Byrne drank. Byrne would give her hell if she knew. But she wouldn't know.

The bartender made jokes and treated her like an old friend though she'd never been here before. Maybe he saw her passing along the street, she thought. More likely, he'd known Pa. Pa had been the sort of person who liked to drink by himself, not the loud kind who treated everybody to a round as soon as he had spare cash. She looked at the stumpy glass holding the scotch and at the tall glass with the water and green stirring rod. The whole set-up didn't look very appetizing. But she had ordered it, and she would drink it.

One of the guys standing near the game machine came over and slid onto the stool next to her. "Hi," he said.

"Hi," she said, pouring the whiskey into the water.

"For a minute, I thought you were going to take that straight." He smiled.

Why do men always assume that any girl alone wants to be picked up? Because she was in a bar didn't mean anything. How did he know she wasn't just a lush? If Byrne were here, she'd know how to get rid of him quickly, painlessly.

One swallow of the drink convinced her that she was not destined to become an alcoholic. With Byrne around, she could drink because Byrne absorbed all her attention and she was safe with her.

The guy ordered himself a beer and winked at the bartender as if to say: Who's the chick?

She paid for the drink and left it unfinished. Outside, she opened her mouth and breathed in cold air. It slid over her tongue, freezing the taste off. Then she hurried up the stairs before some other wise guy started something.

As she walked in the door, it occurred to her that the alcohol on her breath would be terribly suspicious. Of all times in the world to smell from whiskey, this was not one of them.

Her mother was sitting in the bedroom darning a sock, her eyes narrow in the yellow light. Almost midnight. The woman had no business being awake when she had to get Mike off so early in the morning, but she had taken to sleeping less and less. The company of her thoughts did not lend itself to the luxury of sleep.

Paula said hello, knowing she would get a feeble response in return.

She went to her room and dropped onto the bed. Well, if that's how things were going to be, it was a darned good idea to leave. At least with Byrne there was hope and some possibility of happiness.

Mike had borrowed her alarm clock. She heard its ticking in his room. He got up before she did and managed to do a few chores before going to school. Her importance, almost her existence, in the household was being ignored.

She felt, sometimes, that Ma and Mike were conspiring against her as though she had already left them.

Like a protective veil, Paula pulled around her thoughts of Byrne and how Byrne needed her, wanted her. In her imagination she put Byrne's arms about her body and went to sleep with her head on Byrne's shoulder.

Paula went to work the next day, debating with herself whether or not to give two weeks notice. Maybe it would be smarter not to be so hasty about quitting. She went to the personnel manager's office, driven by the thought of having all day, every day, to be with Byrne.

That evening, when the phone rang, Paula let Mike answer it.

"For you," he said, putting the receiver down.

She wanted the family to know there was Byrne in her world. "Who is it? she asked Mike, hoping that Byrne had given her name.

"It's Phil," Mike replied, annoyed that Phil didn't want to speak with him.

"Oh." Disappointed, she went to the phone. Phil's

voice held traces of embarrassment as he asked her to go out with him tonight. Paula knew he had found the courage to phone because of what Byrne had said to him. No, she wouldn't go out. She was sorry, but she didn't feel like it right now. Maybe some other time.

Impatiently she waited for Byrne to call. Maybe she had tried when the line was busy. Paula fidgeted nervously about the house. She pulled out the drawers of the bureau in her room and decided which of her clothes were good enough to bother packing. They all seemed so old or so unsophisticated compared with Byrne's wardrobe. Thank heaven, Byrne hadn't judged by appearances.

When the phone rang again, she made herself stay in the bedroom until Mike answered. "You again," he called, with an edge in his voice.

Paula couldn't risk asking him any questions; she didn't want Byrne on the other end to hear coldness in Mike's tone.

Byrne's voice on the telephone was richer, deeper than in person, the sound soothing as quiet music. They spoke about nothing in particular until Byrne, with amusement, invited Paula to come for a drawing lesson. Just as formally, Paula accepted.

The comfort of having an excuse to go to Byrne made Paula feel wonderful. She almost wished that her mother would ask her where she was going, because to volunteer that information after so many times of running out without a word, would sound too phony.

But nobody asked.

She raced downtown to Byrne and the two of them collapsed with laughter into each other's arms.

"Poor Phil," Paula said, feeling sorry for him while they laughed.

On the couch Paula put her head in Byrne's lap, kicked off her shoes and lifted her feet onto the cushions.

"You know," Byrne said, playing with a strand of Paula's hair. "The more I see of you, the more I realize how much time I've wasted. You make life such a bright, sparkling thing, my darling. I'd forgotten that love could be this way."

Paula took Byrne's hand and brought it to her lips. If she could only keep Byrne like this, so relaxed, so content. Her thoughts drifted into lands of pleasure.

"Will you do something for me?" Paula said, still holding the long fingers.

"You know I will."

"Anything?" Paula asked cautiously.

"Anything."

"Will you do a portrait of me? I don't mean something elaborate. Just a pencil sketch."

Byrne's good humor was indestructible. She bent over and kissed the tip of Paula's nose. "All right, little shrewdy. I don't know what you're getting at, but I'm willing to find out."

Paula just grinned broadly.

"When would you like me to begin this masterpiece?"

"Why not now?" Paula suggested. She did not want to let this mood slip by.

"All right. But don't expect too much. I'm not sure I remember how to hold a pencil."

Paula jumped up and went to get the sketch pads. She set everything in position for Byrne and perched herself on the arm of the couch, much as Byrne had once sat there. She didn't take off her clothes, because she wanted Byrne to do her face only, this time.

Byrne stood before the easel and made preliminary strokes, getting the feel of the pencil, the feel of mastering her craft once again.

Paula sat patiently, glad to have this reason to watch Byrne, uninterrupted. The woman worked slowly at first, as though finding her way along an unfamiliar path. Her eyelids drooped slightly as she considered the angles and shadows of Paula's face. Once, she pushed up her shirt sleeve impatiently as though nothing in the world should interfere between her hands and the creation.

Time went by and gradually faster she worked, with increasing certainty. Byrne's concentration narrowed to a fine point like flame that burned its mark on the paper before her. Standing thus before the easel was for Byrne a perfect setting. The pencil seemed an extension of her arm. Planted firmly on both feet, her very being grew stronger, almost taller. Paula knew she had done the right, the perfect thing to steer Byrne back to her art.

"That's enough for now," Byrne said at last. She put the pencil into her shirt pocket and wiped her forehead with her arm. "We won't have time for anything else if I keep this up." She smiled mischievously.

"Okay," Paula said and stretched the muscles in her neck. "Can I look at it?"

"Wait till it's finished."

She took Paula by the shoulders and steered her into the bedroom. When she had undressed the girl, Byrne massaged her neck, shoulders, back muscles. "You're a very good model," she said. "We must do this more often."

"I'd love it," Paula responded, her words muffled by the pillow pressing against her face.

Soon Byrne's hands turned Paula over and she drew the woman down into her embrace.

After midnight, they lay finally still in the warm darkness, quietly smoking.

"I wish you could stay with me tonight," Byrne said, exhaling a stream of smoke into the silence.

"Then I will."

"No, it's just a whim of mine. I don't think it would be wise to upset your family. They expect you home, I'm sure. We can wait until you've made the proper arrangements."

"Let me tell you something," Paula said, and she couldn't keep the bitterness out of her voice. "My family doesn't give a damn where I go or what I do. When I stopped sitting around the house like a faithful dog, they practically disowned me."

Byrne stubbed out her cigarette and put Paula's into the ashtray. "Poor darling," she murmured, moving closer to her. "It's awfully hard breaking family ties, I know. Try not to be too harsh with them. You know I'll do everything I can to fill the gap for you."

Paula squeezed her close. "You're more important to me than a hundred families. Don't feel sorry for me. Not when I have you. Besides, I'll be here permanently this weekend and they'll never bother me again." Paula heard her own words. They seemed too good to be true.

When Paula finally left for the evening, Byrne did not go to sleep. She went into the living room and stared for a long time at the unfinished portrait. Incredible that this mere wisp of a child could make her return to something she had forsworn so long ago. Her old habit of cynicism tried to laugh it off. Yet the evidence stood clearly on paper. Could it really be, after all these years?

Loyalty to Greta rebelled against the new pleasure and self-knowledge.

How can I be so naive as to think there is still a chance for me? She's just a fling, Byrne thought. I'm kidding myself to take it seriously. But why did I ask her to come live with me? I can have her on any terms I want. What's with me, that I should be looking forward to that colt rollicking through this apartment? Loneliness. Plain everyday loneliness. Pull the wool down for a few weeks.

Disturbed with strange conflict, Byrne went to the bar and poured herself a drink. The stream of her thoughts went on.

But if I'm playing a game with her, why am I sitting here worrying about it? This isn't like you, old girl. How many women have you gone through since Greta went off the deep end? You didn't think twice about them and how glad they were to get away when you let them find out how things stood. So this, too, must be only a pause. Then why are you so eager? Why are you looking forward with a pounding heart? Is it perhaps that you really . . .

Throughout the quiet hours she battled with herself but what use was intellect against a creature who had already found her way to Byrne's emotions?

Part Two

Part Two

8

As the first spray of dawn warmed the sky, Byrne knew that she must face Greta. How could she tell her? What could she impress upon a mind that had withdrawn so far from the ordeal of living? And yet, in fairness to both of the women she loved, she had to do something once and for all that was decisive.

In the bathroom, Byrne scrubbed her face as if to wash away the last fifteen years of semi-living. Had it really been that long? Had the precious time slipped by her this quickly? Until now there had not been a Paula to make time so important.

Wearing pressed slacks and a camel's hair coat, Byrne slipped out of the house. The sudden desire to be free of Greta urged her to action. Small nudges of guilt tried their familiar attempt to imprison her but she thrust them away. For Paula's sake and for her own, she had to try, now, to be a whole person.

The cab took her swiftly uptown in the emptiness of early morning streets. Memories of Greta thrust themselves into her consciousness.

How wonderful it had been at the beginning. That delightful innocence of first passion. Yet more than passion. It had been a whole entanglement of families that flung Greta and herself together.

As the cab whined along the street, Byrne could hear her mother saying: "Greta is coming to help you with your arithmetic."

Greta helped Byrne with homework or stayed with her when Mother went visiting at night or took her to the beach or helped her select a new pair of shoes because Mother never had the time to do any of these things. What good fortune — thought both families — their girls got along so nicely and didn't bother with boys.

They had indeed made a private island of their friendship into which no one could intrude. Little by little, Byrne found excuses to sleep downstairs or Greta found reasons to stay with Byrne all night. They would lie together under the covers and tell each other stories, aware only of the joy each found in the other's company. Then another awareness intruded.

Simply and without question, Greta had leaned over one rainy night and taken Byrne's hand to quiet her fright at the jagged flashes and vibrating thunder. The storm and that first touch of hands tore open their need, spilling each into the arms of the other.

Neither one had said, "I love you."

Why did they need words or promises when there could be nothing to threaten them? The fulfillment of their bodies seemed only one more act among the thousands of acts that united them. When Byrne kissed Greta's hair, it was no different from a peck on the cheek that she might have given her at midday.

If Greta had known others thought this wrong, she had never mentioned it. No words of caution did she give Byrne. Perhaps she had not wanted to foul their beautiful dream by admitting a world that would condemn and separate them. Or perhaps Greta herself did not fully realize the meaning of their closeness.

And Greta could do no wrong.

The goddess who painted like an angel, who knew the answers to Byrne's young questions of life could only be worshipped. The heaven of their bodies' union seemed one more proof that she was truly a goddess.

Byrne could not contain her feelings and had tried to convey to her mother the beauty of Greta's kiss.

To Byrne's surprise, her mother had whirled, cheeks crimson with outrage, and grasped Byrne firmly by the shoulders.

"What are you saying?"

Byrne thought her mother had misunderstood. With youthful desire to share her joy, she explained in lingering detail what happened those nights when she slept with Greta.

"Disgusting animal!" The old-fashioned collar quivered at her mother's throat.

Too late Byrne realized that she must have said something wrong. But what? The sneer and revulsion in her mother's eyes made Byrne leap blindly to Greta's defense. Whatever must be bad, she had to protect Greta from it.

"You don't understand," Byrne stammered, not understanding herself what it could be that made her mother dig fingers into her shoulder as if to tear the skin off her skeleton.

With each phrase that she stammered, Byrne felt herself and Greta sinking deeper into unfamiliar quicksand.

For three days she was locked in the house.

Now her mother took her to school and brought her home and made her take a bath twice a day. She had never before received such attention, yet nothing her mother did could take Byrne's mind off Greta. She would lie awake at night, her arms around the pillow, begging Greta to forgive her.

Worst of all was the thought that she had betrayed Greta. She had to see her. She had to explain. What if she thought she had purposely betrayed her?

There was no way to get out of the locked house.

As the days went by, Byrne's guilt grew beyond control. No matter what the price, she must see Greta just once to explain what had happened, to throw herself at Greta's feet and beg forgiveness. Her tortured mind could form no plan. She could think of only one way to get to see Greta.

The next day Byrne did not meet her mother after school. Instead she ran two blocks to a candy store and phoned Greta's home, praying that Greta herself would answer. Breathlessly she waited for the receiver to be lifted. When the deep voice of Greta's brother said hello, Byrne still did not give up hope.

"Please, Jack, let me speak to Greta."

Jack, though he wanted to, could not help her. Greta had been shipped to their aunt's house in the country.

Byrne's world collapsed. Greta had been taken out of school because of her. She was due to graduate with honors, she had a scholarship to an art school. And Byrne had destroyed it all.

She picked up her schoolbooks and trudged home, not caring if her mother whipped the flesh off her bones or threw her into a dungeon for life. Without Greta there was nothing to live for. Now that she had ruined Greta, too, life became a horrible thing she could not face.

When she reached home, her mother said nothing. She merely smiled at Byrne with the superior knowledge of what Byrne had just learned.

Byrne could not eat the meal placed before her. She could only stare at the plate and think of Greta cooped up so far away from her dreams and ambitions. How could she leave Greta alone and a prisoner?

As the days passed Byrne suffocated in self accusation. Each time she walked out free on the streets, she thought of Greta alone. Each night she went to bed, she recalled Greta's sweet lips and thought of them wasting away unloved. When her mother took her to the movies, it was Greta's face she saw on the screen, her blue eyes gazing sadly down at Byrne.

The nightmare of trying to sleep robbed her nerves of strength. She could not simply sit and do nothing. She must free Greta and make the world know that the fault was hers and not that of her innocent beloved.

Homework went undone. In class, anguished thoughts obliterated the teacher's voice. She barely passed the mid-term examinations. Greta, only Greta lived vividly for her. She lost weight and had to move the buttons on her skirts. Nervous energy alone drove her and her mind focused on one tiny burning point — free Greta.

Until finally Byrne could no longer live without doing it.

In the middle of the night, she took from the savings bowl, money equivalent to the allowance that had been denied her the past two months. She knew that the authorities would question a fifteen-year-old girl trying to buy a train ticket at one in the morning. She would have to wait until daylight. Carefully she unlatched the door and slipped into the hallway. For the rest of the night she hid in the basement. Then, when daylight broke, she rode to the train station before her mother discovered that she was missing.

To see Greta again! To look at the slender fingertips that seemed to caress without touching. To hear the light footstep and the singing voice. Just one more minute with Greta and she would be content to die.

And a minute would be all they would have. Byrne knew that her mother would know where she had gone.

At the depot she discovered that she had just enough money for a one-way ticket. Tall men pushing carts of luggage smiled at her and an elderly gentleman helped her up the steps into the train. She found a seat near the window and prayed that the train would start before her mother arrived and came on board to look for her.

The trip was only an hour long and Byrne knew the route by heart. She had often travelled it with Greta during Christmas and summer vacations.

Listening to the clicking of the wheels, Byrne tried to relax. She watched the leafless trees whip by and tried not to think how Greta might receive her.

Maybe Greta wouldn't want to see her. She couldn't blame her if she didn't. But Greta had to understand. She couldn't go on for the rest of her life thinking that Byrne had said ugly things about their love.

After an eternity of waiting, the train slowed and stopped at her station. She listened to the conductor call the name out like a great judge pronouncing her doom.

In the station house she tried to warm herself at a pot-bellied stove while she waited for the bus that went to the house. The stench of old cigars reminded her of Greta's uncle. He would look down from his great height over the cigar that stuck straight out from between his lips. He would understand and help her.

The old bus rattled to a halt behind the tracks and Byrne ran to board it, knowing that she would still have to wait ten minutes before the driver started on the return trip.

Bouncing along the dirt road she looked out at the brown stubble that grew along the hillside. For miles above her the gray sky drearily stretched. The desolate hills had long since dropped their blooms and even the occasional rabbits that hopped quickly off the road seemed lonely.

When the driver came to her stop, Byrne held her breath. Her legs were unsteady things that balanced her body with effort, but she went bravely down the gravel path toward the clapboard house.

Maybe Greta would be around in the back sorting apples. Byrne hurried along the side and peered down between the slanted doors that opened into the basement. No light was there.

"Greta?" she said softly.

Silence answered her.

She went down the steps and looked around, hoping that perhaps Greta had not heard her.

Only coils of garden hose and bulging potato sacks met her sight.

Greta must be upstairs. Maybe she was in her room on the top floor that looked outward over the hills and toward the city.

Unhappily Byrne retraced her steps and walked with uncertain determination back to the front door.

She climbed the crooked steps and listened to them squeak beneath her feet. Then she rapped on the screen door and waited. Her breath caught in her throat and her heart knocked wildly in her chest. If only she had wings to sweep Greta up and fly away from here before the adults could swarm down on them. She still did not understand why these terrible things had happened as a result of the loveliness she and Greta had shared. How could it be sinful to be so content?

Byrne heard the heavy footsteps of Greta's uncle and crossed her fingers fervently.

"Hello, little girl," he said in the slow voice that could hide surprise. He always called her "little girl" and Byrne felt encouraged.

"May I come in?" she said in a thin voice that trembled with breathlessness.

He opened the door and tapped a long cigar ash to the ground. "Of course you can come in."

Byrne wondered why he didn't ask what she was doing here or where her mother was or anything. She came onto the inside porch where the old wicker chairs seemed to beckon her gently.

"Had a good trip?" He made easy conversation while she took off her coat. "This time of year makes mighty bitter traveling." He smiled amiably and the red veins in his cheeks crinkled.

Byrne let him take her coat, then followed him into the spacious kitchen.

"Nobody's home but me," he chatted. "But I can make as good a cup of coffee as anyone."

The question that leaped to Byrne's frantic mind remained unspoken. She had to conduct herself like a lady. So far, Uncle John was on her side. At least he wasn't calling her all kinds of names and acting like she was a poisonous witch.

After he placed two heavy mugs on the table, Byrne asked, "Isn't Greta here?"

"Oh, she's staying here, all right," he said gently. "She's not here this morning, though. Her Aunt Nell took her over to visit with the Regans. Everybody seems to think it's time Greta got herself a husband, you know." He stirred sugar into his coffee as if the words he'd just said were ordinary words, not the most horrible things that Byrne could hear.

Byrne knew the Regan boys. One was fat and the other one fatter. They were wealthy and would inherit a lot of money some day. It didn't make any difference to the family which one Greta married, so long as she married one of them. The vision of Greta, who could not stand the two boys, being forced to marry one of them horrified Byrne.

"Oh, Uncle John," she blurted. "You've got to help her!"

He searched her face with dark and kind blue eyes. He seemed to find and understand the earnestness in Byrne that had prompted her outburst.

"Everybody's got their minds made up," he said, striking a large match and moving its flame to the cigar.

"But Greta doesn't want to marry either of the Regan boys." Even if Greta didn't love Byrne, she wouldn't want one of those two.

"You don't think so?" "It was her own idea that her Aunt Nell take her there this morning."

Byrne's mind went blank. Why would Greta want to do a thing like that? What must she be suffering? What horrible tortures could push her into that kind of decision?

"Greta's almost eighteen," Uncle John continued. "I suspect she knows how to make up her own mind."

Maybe Uncle John didn't know what the trouble

was. Maybe no one had told him what had happened between her and Greta. If he did know, would he understand why Greta would want to drive herself into such a corner? If she told him, would he help? If she told him, he might throw her out. If she didn't tell him, he could never help Greta.

Byrne had to take the chance. For Greta's sake.

She took a long drink of coffee and then explained to him as simply as she could everything that had happened.

He listened to her story without interruption and Byrne didn't spare herself. She repeated what her mother had said and how she had been treated as a result. She emphasized that none of this had been Greta's fault. That the blame must be hers alone.

When she had finished her story, Uncle John put down his cigar and folded the stained fingers around the strap of his overalls.

"You know," he said, "when you spend your life tending animals, you get to respect nature."

She looked at him with question, moving her palm nervously along the nicked table top.

"The first law of nature," he said, "is that animals and men and all living things should reproduce their kind. I guess that's all I can see wrong with what you're telling me. It doesn't lead anywhere except into a blind alley, seems to me. Pretty girls, strong girls like you and Greta should have homes and raise families someday."

Byrne started to protest. She had always expected to have a family. That was something taken for granted, even if not particularly wanted. It seemed like something you just did; everybody had a family. Why couldn't she love Greta and have a family too? Why should one get in the way of the other?

Yet Uncle John said that it would and she trusted him enough to believe in his judgment.

"Then if Greta has to get married," Byrne persisted, "that means I have to get married too?"

"Right," he nodded.

"So she'll marry one of the Regan boys and I'll marry the other." A triumphant feeling floated through her. This way, Greta wouldn't have to suffer alone. If they could both be married and have houses across the street from each other or maybe apartments in the same building, she could still see her every day and things would be all right.

Uncle John said, "Maybe in a few years. You're still kind of young for marrying, you know."

A few years? Separated from Greta all that time!

In school she had learned that there were certain states in the union where you could get married at fourteen, and she was a year older than that. She told Uncle John.

"Just the same, I think you're safer waitin'." He smiled quietly.

But the plan was already forming in Byrne's mind. The happy prospect of being near Greta again relieved some of her tension. She finished the remains of her coffee, enjoying the warmth of it in her stomach.

She sat back against the high wooden chair and inhaled the warm odor of preserves cooking on the stove. Greta would be back soon and she could tell her all about how wonderful things would be for them again. Uncle John didn't press her into further conversation. He, too, sat back, contemplating things from behind the whirls of smoke that rose lazily from his cigar.

At last they both heard the crunch of footsteps coming toward the house. Once again Byrne's nerves jumped but the anticipation of seeing Greta held her frozen to the chair. She clutched the edge of the table top and turned her face toward the doorway.

Aunt Nell came in first, her small mouth tied in a tiny knot of satisfaction. Behind her, Greta ambled slowly as though drawn along by an invisible rein, her gaze fastened on the tips of her shoes. Byrne waited excitedly for her to look up.

"What's she doing here?" Aunt Nell snorted.

The tone made Greta look up.

Byrne, grinning happily with the joy of the new plan, burst her beaming gladness upon Greta. She wanted to run to her, hug her, assure her that everything was going to be all right.

Then Byrne saw in Greta's eyes a strange thing that she had never seen before. They didn't shine, those eyes. A dulling film seemed to have dropped like a curtain before them. She barely seemed to know Byrne. It took some moments before she said hello.

Uncle John said some combination of magic words that calmed his wife's annoyance, but Byrne did not hear him speak. She could concentrate only on Greta. With a burst of enthusiasm, she rushed out of the chair and over to her darling, wanting to fight her

137

way past that unfamiliar curtain and back into the loveliness and warmth that had always been her Greta.

Greta smiled stiffly, as though she were meeting Byrne for the first time.

"I'm getting married," she said in a voice that seemed to float over Byrne's head.

"Yes, I know." Byrne tried to be enthusiastic. "That's wonderful. And I'm going to get married too." She smiled encouragingly, hoping Greta would change back into her old self, that she would reach out with the familiar tenderness and laugh softly with her.

Aunt Nell started to say something calculated to bite at Byrne, but her husband managed to lead her away into the parlor. Byrne was alone with Greta at last.

The two girls looked at each other wordlessly, though Byrne felt that she had a million things to say all at once.

"Greta, darling, it was all my fault," she whispered. "I didn't mean to do you any harm."

"Your fault?" Greta repeated. "I'm older than you are. You didn't know what you were doing, but I did." She couldn't seem to look at Byrne directly. Her gaze sought fugitive places up on the ceiling or over at the sink.

"What did we do, Greta, that was so terrible?" Byrne insisted, aching to reach out and have Greta take her hand.

Greta laced her fingers tightly together. "We sinned," she murmured without strength. "I wanted to protect you and I led you into the path of damnation instead."

138

"What are you talking about?" Byrne said. She recognized Greta's words as an echo of her Aunt Nell. How could Greta believe that anything as wonderful as what they had done would be sin?

But Greta's mind roamed far away from every argument Byrne offered. She seemed to have opened the door and stepped into an unreachable place where Byrne could not follow. Byrne felt an inkling of fear, for the first time. Not for herself and not because of the thing that was supposed to be sin. Yet that fear crawled along under the surface of her skin and make her cold. This Greta was not the Greta she had known two months before. Byrne didn't know what the difference was; all she could see and understand was that something horrible closed Greta away from her.

And Byrne knew it was her own fault.

The marriage took place that month. Everybody seemed anxious to have it as quickly as possible.

When the wedding ring was securely on Greta's finger, the restrictions that had prevented Byrne from seeing her beloved were relaxed.

Of course she was living in the country now and Byrne could get away to her only on weekends. It was merely a question of patience. She went out with the other Regan boy, the thinner one. She dressed nicely and did everything to please him, hoping that he would ask her to marry him.

She watched Greta to see what it was like to be a good housewife. Greta seemed to take on the chore without difficulty. She cleaned her new home and baked cakes and floated around as if nothing touched her. Yet everything did. Everything was getting in the way of their natural conversations. The wedding ring twinkled like a diamond wall between them, teamed up with that hateful garnet solitaire she wore, a present from her mother, that Greta would never give up. Byrne prayed for that far away feeling to disappear. Instead it seemed to be getting worse. Greta hardly laughed anymore. When something pleased her, an odd smile would flit across her lips, and disappear. One day Byrne realized that the unfamiliar odor surrounding Greta was the smell of whiskey.

They never talked about the same things anymore either. Uneasily, Byrne began to think that maybe Greta hated her.

One Saturday, when Greta's husband had gone to town for the week's shopping, Byrne confronted her.

"I've got to know the truth," she pleaded. She had taken Greta into the living room and forced her to sit down on the couch and give complete attention.

"I've got to know," Byrne choked, "how you feel about me."

She waited for the dread words to stab her ears.

Greta said, "I'm very thirsty, dear. Can't I have a drink first?"

Impatiently Byrne got out the bottle and filled two glasses. She watched with unhappiness as Greta emptied hers and refilled it twice.

"Don't you want to tell me?" Byrne said. "Anything would be better than this not knowing. Do you hate me for what I've done? Do you?"

Greta put down her glass. She seemed to be mustering the forces that had scattered inside her.

"I love you, darling," she whispered. "There is nothing in this world that means anything to me except you."

Thankfully Byrne relaxed against the over-stuffed sofa. "And I adore you. Worship you."

Before either of them knew what had happened, they were in each other's embrace, kissing away the tortured months that had kept them apart.

It did not seem strange to Byrne that they made love in hurried intervals. She was grateful for Greta's kisses whenever she could get them. By now the textbooks in the library had revealed to her the meaning of their feelings, and she realized too that Greta had married as a protection against the evil name that went with their kind of loving.

Still Byrne knew that she had committed irreparable damage. Though Greta responded with the ecstasy that Byrne had come to expect, she did not show any exuberance or even the suggestion of happiness at other times. Only when they were in each other's arms did she come alive.

Greta began to bulge out of her clothes, not seeming to care about her appearance anymore. The silken mane hung in tangled masses around the housedress that gaped open at the strained buttonholes. The grace and the beauty that had been Greta decayed. Her carelessness spread through the house, too. Empty whiskey bottles rolled beneath the furniture. Byrne began to sense in herself an outrageous feeling of shame that she struggled vainly to subdue. To hear Isaac Regan grumble about his wife's sloppiness hurt Byrne.

She tried to tell herself that Greta was bored with living so far away in the country. So Byrne brought her drawing equipment in the hope of reviving the dull spirits.

And Greta did begin to draw. She filled pages and pages with strange heads as though she was trying to loosen from within herself an anguish that could find no words. As the months drew into a year, Greta stopped doing anything else except painting and drinking. She carried a full glass of whiskey with her constantly and sometimes Byrne argued with her about it, only to hear Greta laugh a strange laugh that made no sense.

The biggest shock of all came when Byrne entered the house one day to discover Greta in the process of cutting off her hair.

She sat, not before a mirror, but in the kitchen, snipping at the back of her head, hacking jagged scars in the beautiful thick blonde fleece.

Horrified, Byrne snatched the scissors away from her. It was too late. As Greta looked up in mute helplessness, Byrne realized for the first time how much damage Greta had done to herself, not just to the hair. The smooth complexion had lost its rosiness. The fine line of jaw had begun to sag into a slovenly mass of flesh. Byrne felt sick. She put the scissors back into the drawer and fought to ward off the depression that pressed into her mind.

She loved Greta. She would always love Greta. A fierce loyalty bound her to this poor woman whom she had so innocently betrayed. If it weren't for her own stupidity, Greta would not be suffering so. If Byrne had not interfered, Greta would be in New York, making a name for herself in the art world, living a rich existence, full of the happiness of accomplishment. Byrne alone was responsible for the destruction of this once wonderful being, and she must stay with her. At the least, she could help fend off people's inevitable accusing looks and degrading words — cutting, painful words that even Isaac never ceased to say.

By the time Byrne graduated from high school, Isaac had started divorce proceedings.

Byrne shared the shame, and it seared through her pride. At the same time, she was glad. Isaac was willing to give Greta a great deal of money if she would not fight the separation, and she could go to New York. Byrne would live with her there. She was eighteen now. At last no one in the world could stop her from doing what she wanted. Maybe, if they lived together, away from reminders of blame and guilt, Greta would regain her health.

What encouraged Byrne most was Greta's desire to live with her. In the midst of her detachment and withdrawn isolation, this one last remnant of enthusiasm still appeared.

Byrne had an apartment ready by the time Greta's divorce came through.

Since there was no problem of money, Byrne had all the time in the world to lavish on her beloved.

After breakfast, she would say, "Let's take a ride up to Bear Mountain."

But Greta would sit in the armchair and hug her knees up to her chest. She stared out the window at nothing in particular, just far away.

"Well, how about the zoo?"

Whatever Byrne suggested met with no response. With a sigh, Byrne would pick up a book and try to interest herself in stories of other women's lives.

Only at night did Greta come alive. When they

143

had climbed into bed, she would fling herself on Byrne and passionately dig her teeth into the soft flesh of her girl's belly. Byrne, mistaking this for ecstasy, thrilled to the pain at first. Yet she could not bring herself to treat Greta with anything except gentleness.

They would spend the night in lovemaking. Nothing seemed to satisfy Greta. Content to sleep during the day, her energies focused in wild excitement when she held Byrne within naked reach. And Byrne accepted this ardent possession, not daring to admit that it did not satisfy her, that it left her feeling base and without gladness.

She recognized that lolling around the house all day drained her energies into a pool of boredom. She needed to do other things besides sketch. The world sat outside on her doorstep, waiting to be explored. She ached to experience it. Nothing she could say or do excited Greta into wanting to share this with her.

Byrne took to going to the movies alone. If it was a comedy she would sit in the darkness laughing to herself, terribly aware of having no one to share the fun.

One evening Byrne came home to find Greta huddled in a corner, staring up at her like an angry animal.

"You said I could go," Byrne protested.

Without a word Greta leaped at her. She pounced upon Byrne with surprising agility for a woman of her weight. Byrne could not protect herself without hurting Greta. She crossed her forearms in front of her face and let Greta's fists pound and the nails claw until the woman was out of breath.

"You don't love me," Greta panted in a furious whisper.

"Of course I do." She lowered her arms and sought Greta's eyes. They looked beyond Byrne and seemed to be speaking to someone far away. Tears rose and welled over on Byrne's cheeks. She could no longer deny to herself that Greta's mind was unbalanced.

Greta did not become increasingly worse. True, she began to insist that she felt stupid in a dress, yet she would occasionally go out for a walk with Byrne or listen to the radio. She made just enough conversation to permit Byrne to believe that she didn't need to be hospitalized.

And, of course, there were her magnificent paintings. She would sometimes look at Byrne's work and, with rapid short strokes, show her exactly what was wrong. Then and only then would Byrne feel a glimmer of the once sharp intelligence.

Byrne continued to live this weird existence of alternating hope and loneliness. She didn't question that there could be such a thing as real companionship for her. Greta was her first responsibility, especially now that a psychiatrist had diagnosed her case as incurable.

Their apartment became for Byrne a chamber of horrors. Two Chinese lamps that she had bought were long since smashed in one of Greta's fits. Deep holes in the plaster reminded her of the violence always lying dormant, even when the two of them were sitting quietly watching television.

It never occurred to Byrne that she should have a separate apartment where she could be alone occasionally and pull her battered spirits together. The idea came very innocently one day when a young girl in the supermarket started to talk to her.

They were both pushing carts along the frozen foods counter when the girl picked up a package of deviled crabs and said to Byrne, "Gee, I wonder if this brand is any good. Have you ever used it?"

Byrne looked at the dark curling hair and the bright vivacious eyes and felt an overwhelming desire to make ordinary conversation with an ordinary person.

"I've used them many times," Byrne said eagerly. "The trick is to get them good and brown." She wished she could invite her over and show her how to prepare them.

The girl thanked her and strolled on, leaving Byrne to realize more strongly than ever how impossible it would be to make friends with anybody because of Greta's condition.

She began to look in the "apartments for rent" column, hardly realizing her motives.

Greta had taken to sleeping more than ever. Whole days slipped by, lost to her. Soon Byrne rented a place on Eleventh Street, knowing that if she did not get away, her own sanity might be threatened too.

From this it was only a small step to having visitors. Casual friends at first, who chatted about current events, then gradually, a woman whom Byrne would take into her arms, forgetting her past for a moment, ignoring the anchor that dragged at her heart.

How many women passed in and out of her life like this? Byrne always managed to let them know she could give nothing permanent. Susan . . . Phyllis . . . Rachel . . . They all came and went like sea shells rolling up on a beach, then sliding back into the ocean . . .

Byrne had not expected ever to meet anyone like Paula. When she did, her safely sealed heart knocked against the doors of its prison, demanding to be freed.

No one had insisted the way Paula insisted on her right to love. Byrne, for all her responsibilities and loyalties to Greta, had succumbed.

There was nothing left but to face the idea of putting Greta into the hands of someone who could care for her properly. A nurse of some sort would stay with Greta during the time when Byrne must be with Paula.

For two weeks Byrne interviewed women until she found the right person for Greta, but Greta was not so detached from life that she did not know what was happening.

She looked at Byrne with wide eyes that could not comprehend and said, "Why don't you want to live with me any more?" Her voice fluttered around Byrne with helplessness.

"I'll see you very often," Byrne replied and struggled to keep a bright expression on her lips.

"Where will you be living?" Greta folded her hands childlike on her lap. Years of sitting had made a caricature of her body. The warm, woman's curves lay hidden beneath pads of fat and flab now.

"Not too far." Byrne tried to reassure her, knowing it was hopeless.

"Will you show me where?" She tilted her head up with pleading. The gesture reminded Byrne of a dog tied outside the store waiting for its master.

"Of course."

"Take me now?" she begged eagerly.

Byrne had not the strength to deny her request. She brought Greta down to her apartment and watched her wander from room to room, as though she were searching for a corner in which to curl up and hide herself.

Byrne took her by the hand and led her back into the living room.

"See?" she said, pointing to Greta's painting above the bookshelf. "I've got you with me all the time."

Byrne reached in vain for some response of pleasure. Greta's eyes remained as ever dull.

"Can I come and visit you sometimes?" A tremor as of tears shook in her voice.

Instinctively Byrne pulled Greta into her arms. "Of course you can," she whispered, struggling to sound cheerful. "You can come here any time you want."

Now Greta smiled.

"I'll wait for you," Greta said. "I always want to wait for you."

Byrne brought her back to her own apartment and then left hurriedly. She went to a small dark bar and drank to quiet the tearing thoughts and poisonous guilt that pulled at her with such pain.

Part Three

9

Memories of the past fading, Byrne sat stiffly in
the taxi, trying not to think of how Greta would
respond to the news that she must go to a
sanitarium.

Her desire to be with Paula was not the only
factor influencing Byrne's decision to send Greta
away. Byrne had finally forced herself to face the
issue, to recognize Greta's warped instincts, her
savagery, her pathological loneliness. Byrne had
finally steeled herself to the inevitable task. She could
no longer run away from the problem or continue to

make excuses for Greta. Both women had to be considered.

Her first responsibility, Byrne decided, was to the living. The semi-living must be attended to in whatever way was most humane. She could no longer allow Greta to rule her life.

Dear Paula — she thought it was all so simple. Thank heaven, she knew nothing of the pain.

Handing a bill to the cab driver, Byrne got out and went resolutely up to Greta's apartment.

Byrne smiled to herself as the nurse opened the door. How easily Greta had managed to slip out from beneath this woman's surveillance whenever she felt like it!

"It's all right, Mattie," Byrne said. "You can go out for an hour or so. I want to be alone with her."

Greta was sitting on the floor, a sketch pad tilted on her knees. She didn't say one word to Byrne until Mattie had left the apartment.

Then she broke the charcoal stick in half and offered a piece to Byrne.

She sat down on the floor beside Greta and kissed her lightly on the cheek.

"How are you, dear?" Byrne said, uncertain of how much to tell Greta about the sanitarium. She wasn't so detached and unaware of things that the men could come and take her without any previous explanation. Byrne had to make Greta realize that she wasn't being shipped off like a dead thing. Yet, wasn't that the real truth?

Greta kissed her back fiercely. She hooked her arms around Byrne's neck in a tight grip and pulled Byrne hard to her.

"You love me," she whispered. "I know you love me, even if you don't want to see me very much any more."

Byrne could find no words with which to soothe her. She herself was struggling through a morass of emotions that bludgeoned her sensibilities with a frantic desire to give in completely, once more, to this woman whose mind she had helped shatter. But the shining image of Paula saved Byrne. She could not betray Paula as she had betrayed this woman so long ago. Paula must be given a chance to live without the perpetual threat and hurt of Byrne's guilt hovering over them.

"Darling," Byrne said gently. "How would you like to go on a nice little trip?" She felt Greta's breath against her neck and knew that she wasn't listening. "Wouldn't it be pleasant?" she continued. "Some place where there is grass and trees and a pretty park where you can walk around instead of in this apartment?"

She loosened Greta's fingers from around her and made her look directly into her face.

"Wouldn't you like a change from the city for a while?"

Greta eyed her warily. "Are you coming, too?" she asked in a voice that held obvious, little-girl fear.

Byrne hesitated. "I'll take you there," she said soothingly. "Then I'll show you everything and help you make some friends."

"I don't want to go without you!" She lunged forward again and clung to Byrne. "Don't leave me," she begged in a small voice. "Please don't leave me all alone."

Byrne almost weakened. She could not bear to hear this desolation but she had made the decision and she knew it was the right one.

"I won't let you leave me," Greta said loudly. Her panting breath bathed Byrne in its desperation.

Byrne let the woman cling to her for a while. She felt herself being pulled down into the core of Greta's sickness. A drowning sensation overwhelmed her. How could a love such as theirs decay into this fantastic nightmare?

All that saved her from being immersed and lost like Greta was the insistent image of Paula's young enthusiasm. She closed her eyes tightly and recalled the sweet kisses they had shared so tenderly. She remembered the innocent joy and the expectation of a full life that surrounded Paula's every word, her every movement.

Did she not have a right to this life with Paula? Was she compelled to sink with Greta into a dismal nothingness? Must she pay and pay until death, for words spoken in good faith so long ago, to a mother who could not understand?

Once again Byrne tried to disengage herself from Greta's strangling fingers.

"You can't leave me. I won't let you." Greta began to beat against Byrne's chest with violent blows. Her fists pounded, as though to batter away the decision, the words that would send her away.

Byrne grabbed Greta's wrists and tried to calm her, but the vision of being taken from Byrne blazed wildly in Greta's eyes and she tore herself loose with intense strength.

"You can't go . . . You can't go away . . ." She

grabbed Byrne's shoulders and shook her without awareness.

Byrne shoved Greta away. The force of her push sent Greta skidding across the floor. She banged into the wall and her head hit the plaster with a sickening thud.

Byrne swallowed hard and stood up. She couldn't bear her own behavior but what way out was left for her? She tried desperately to be objective. No one with any sense of responsibility could allow a person like Greta to remain outside a hospital. The danger she presented both to herself and to others required the skills and facilities of protective medical surroundings. She would find for Greta the best that money could buy. Greta would have all the luxuries available, but she must no longer be allowed to roam free.

The best thing would be to leave her now to sink back into her usual lethargy. Byrne hesitated to let her remain alone. If only Mattie would return she could go.

Greta sat there against the wall, her lips wet and glistening.

"I know you want to lock me away," she said. "I'd rather die first. And take you with me."

She made no move to get up. She slumped with her legs spread apart, only the toes of her shoes moving to show that life remained in her.

Byrne adjusted her blouse and noted that the top button had been ripped off. She sat down on a chair, resigned to waiting for the nurse.

It seemed hours before the woman got back. By the time her key turned in the lock, Greta had once again subsided into the dull unspeaking mass of flesh that she was most often.

Unable to look at her, afraid the sight of her would drain her remaining strength, Byrne hastily left the apartment.

Byrne stood outside in the bitter daylight, letting the wind burn its coldness into her skin. Then she started slowly to walk up the street, knowing that there were many things still to be accomplished before she could live decently with Paula.

First of all, she must square with Phil. She found a phone and caught him at home before he left for work. He said he would come right over.

Steeling herself for the job ahead, Byrne went slowly to answer his knock.

He sat down reluctantly.

"There's no point in wasting words," she began. "Or letting you down slowly. Please listen to what I have to say and if you hate me for it, I won't blame you."

Phil waited, his dark face pale with anxiety.

"It's about Paula, of course. Paula and myself, to be exact." Early morning buses rumbled somewhere on the street, pulling the rest of the world into its daily cycle.

"You came here the other day to ask why Paula isn't interested in you any more," Byrne continued. "I'm the answer. Much as I hated it to happen — for many reasons — she fell in love with me. I tried to discourage her. Now I don't want to anymore and I'm going to do my best to keep her, Phil. I only hope you'll accept what I tell you and not cause her more pain than she already feels. We both admire and love you but this is the way things are. I wanted you to know."

Phil managed to light a cigarette. He dropped the match into an ashtray and watched its dying smoke curl upward and fade. "I brought her here to impress you," he said. "What kind of a lousy world is this anyway? My own aunt. I wouldn't listen when the family talked about you that way."

"Believe me, I'd a thousand times rather have her be sensible enough to realize that you're a much better bargain than I am. All I can say is that I won't stand in Paula's way if she changes her mind."

"If that's how you feel, why don't you help her change it?"

Byrne smiled gently. "I'm no martyr."

"Well, neither am I. So just remember, I'm going to stick around every bit as long as you do."

"Good."

He squashed out his cigarette and went to the door. "Thanks anyway for telling me."

10

That Saturday morning Paula took out the old valise and set it on the floor beside her closet. Excitement thrilled her as she folded her favorite wool skirt and laid it neatly in the bag. Ma had resumed her usual domestic tasks and it almost seemed as though her father had only gone away for a visit. Paula couldn't help but expect the door to open at any minute and see him come walking in.

Paula chose another skirt, put her three best blouses on top of them and filled in the remaining space with underwear and toilet articles. She didn't have any shoes worth bothering about but tucked one pair of heels in just to be safe. Then she placed her green dress carefully on top and snapped the suitcase closed. If she had forgotten anything, she could always come back for it.

This was Mike's first day at the paint store and he had already left for work. Paula wished she had been able to say goodbye to him. Being alone like this with Ma was awkward and just to walk out on her as if she were only going to the store for a can of soup would be horrible.

She tried to think of something adequate to say but the words sounded stilted even in her mind. If anything, Paula didn't want to be phoney. She merely wanted to be as simple, as natural as she was in her relationship with Byrne.

Ma had seen her packing but she pretended not to notice. Paula wished that she would protest, not let her walk out without a word.

She brought the valise into the hallway and took a glass of water to give Ma a chance to say something if she wanted to. The woman continued to shell peas into a dish and all Paula heard was the soft plink they made against the crockery.

"I wish," Paula began. No matter how much of a mess she made, she had to say something. "I wish it hadn't happened," she said, conscious that she conveyed no meaning. "I'll call you every so often and you'll get my check in the mail each week."

"Keep your money," her mother said with effort. She didn't look up at Paula but kept her eyes on what she was doing. "We don't want your money."

Paula didn't have the heart to fight. She wouldn't insist on winning her point but she would send the

159

check anyway. Certainly, her mother wouldn't tear it up.

"Tell Mike so long." Picking up the suitcase, she escaped from the apartment.

The happiness of going to Byrne was dimmed by the memory of her mother's words. It isn't fair, she told herself. I can't do only the things she wants me to do. I'm old enough to make my own decisions.

Byrne had the door ajar and Paula dragged the suitcase in without knocking. Still in pajamas, Byrne looked more delicate than usual. Paula dropped the valise and buried her face in the warm-smelling material. Byrne let her cling for awhile, stroking the head and kissing it gently, soothing away the turmoil that spun inside of Paula.

"Is that everything?" she said at last, looking at the suitcase on the floor and wrinkling her forehead.

"Yes," said Paula, blushing. "You probably won't even like what's inside."

"Probably not," Byrne agreed with a soft laugh. "Let's see."

Self-consciously, Paula opened the lid and stood back to watch Byrne as she bent over and lifted out the things one by one. She held up the green dress and said, "I think we should keep this for sentimental reasons. Undoubtedly it's your pride and joy."

Paula was grateful for Byrne's teasing. She knew that the woman was doing this only to give her mind some rest from the tearing emotions that pulled at her heart.

"And this," Byrne continued, shaking a blouse out of its folds, "is a very rare article indeed. These long collar points simply fascinate me." She sat back on

160

the floor and crossed her legs. "I have a very fine idea, if you're up to it," Byrne said. "Supposing I get dressed and we go uptown to shop? A budding commercial artist should start to exercise her talent for color and design."

Paula came to sit on the carpet beside her. "Oh, hold me," she said, closing her eyes to fight away the burning. "Hold me."

Byrne put her arms around Paula and held her tightly. "You're mine," she whispered, "and I won't let anything make you unhappy. Ever."

Paula struggled to pull herself together. Bringing those other burdens into her new life with Byrne wasn't fair. She vowed to herself never to mention them again and she began by thrusting them from her mind now.

"Clothes," she said, making herself concentrate on this business of being well dressed. "I've only been in those stores once. To get a graduation present the whole class chipped in for."

"Well, today we're going to find a graduation present for you. Let's hope we agree on what you should wear."

She looked at Paula to see if it was all right to let go of her yet. Paula helped her by getting up and seating herself on the reading chair. "Hurry." Paula grinned. "I can't wait to pick out my trousseau." She winked grandly at Byrne who made a teasingly sour expression.

Paula wanted to watch her dress but she couldn't move from the chair. The thought of shopping in expensive stores frightened her a little. She would have to get used to this new level of living. In time, they would go to the theater and fancy restaurants,

161

spending what amounted to more than a week's salary in one night. How many millions of women would ache to be in her place?

I've got so much to learn, Paula thought. So many little things that Byrne takes for granted. But Byrne hasn't always been rich. She'll help me.

Byrne came back wearing a pale blue suit that showed off the line of her leg beneath the material. The way Byrne held herself, erect but with the ease of polished grooming, made Paula breathless. In a pair of alligator pumps, she stood taller than most men. Paula thought, "This creature is mine. All mine, and I'll have to work hard to deserve her."

"Ready?" Byrne said as she flung on a dark blue coat.

They left the suitcase in the middle of the room and taxied up Fifth Avenue into the Saturday shopping crowds.

Byrne had charge accounts in half a dozen smart stores. She led Paula from rack to rack, making her feel the different materials, showing her the advantages of different textures and how to match or mix them. Byrne wasn't trying to make Paula over into her own image. The pastel shades did not go well with Paula's dark brown eyes. She looked better in chestnut and electric blue and other strong tones. As she tried things on in the dressing room — a whole dressing room to herself without the smell of other bodies pushing and struggling around her — she found herself standing straighter automatically. I can be part of Byrne's world, she thought. All I need is a little time.

In the mirror she watched the reflection of Byrne's face and noted the smile of approval. Byrne's appreciation was all she wanted. That would give her the courage to do anything.

By three in the afternoon, both women were exhausted. They rode up to Central Park and went into one of the restaurants which Paula had seen advertised in magazines that catered to rich people.

Byrne, at ease as though they were going into a cafeteria, smiled greeting at the hostess who led them to a table.

Paula stared at the menu and remembered that she was not supposed to care about the prices. "I'll have a steak," she said to Byrne.

"Shrimp cocktail first?"

"No," Paula said, recalling the skinny shrimp in an Italian restaurant, that had nearly killed her.

Byrne ordered for them both and Paula was glad that she did not ask for a highball. Paula never wanted to see whiskey again because to drink meant to be unhappy and Paula had no intention of being unhappy or allowing Byrne to be.

They chatted about little things. Sitting across the white tablecloth from this beautiful creature, she felt that everyone must be staring at them. Filled with pride, Paula basked in Byrne's company.

When the waiter brought Byrne's shrimp cocktail, Paula stared at it with surprise. "They're whales," she said.

Promptly Byrne said to the waiter, "Please bring another one."

He nodded and departed.

"Next time I'll know better," Paula laughed.

The experience of dinner made Paula feel as if she had never before eaten in her life. Food had always been something just a little greasy or a little too spiced. Accustomed to that, she never thought about the possibility of dining for pleasure. Even Sunday dinners were dull repetitions of roast chicken or Virginia ham. She was sick to death of both.

Placed before her on its shining platter, her steak oozed succulent juice. Byrne let her concentrate on the meal — which Paula found impossible not to do; experience made her feel like a child confronted with a new and exciting toy.

"It's very strange," Paula said after dessert. She leaned back in the chair, satisfied, a bit too full, but happy. "All your life you try to believe that money isn't everything. But aside from love, I think it really is."

"You're drunk on cream pie," Byrne laughed. She herself had relaxed from the full dinner and was languidly stirring sugar into her coffee.

"I'm drunk on everything. Cream pie, clothes, taxi rides. Mostly you."

"Stay that way." Byrne lit both their cigarettes and Paula noticed a man watching them curiously from his own table across the room.

Irritated, she wondered what he was looking at but decided not to call Byrne's attention to it.

Byrne must have caught the sudden annoyance on her face because she followed the direction of Paula's glance.

"Don't let it bother you," Byrne said in a low voice. "After a while you'll get used to it. Pretty soon, you won't notice it at all."

"But why?" Paula said. "We don't look like freaks. I think he's jealous because you're not with him," Paula said decidedly.

"Maybe that's it," Byrne agreed. "Whatever the reason, let's not spoil our dinner because of him."

"Agreed."

But Paula couldn't regain her previous comfort and contentment. She felt an itch in the side of her head where the man was looking.

They finally left the restaurant and took a cab back home.

"We'll stay in tonight," Byrne said. "I don't think either one of us is up to an evening on the town."

She found an old pair of jeans for Paula to wear and put on her charcoal slacks because Paula told her how much she liked them.

The realization that she didn't have to leave tonight, that she would not be returning to that now loveless and cold apartment, blew Paula into a lightness of heart that made her feel she could float right out the window and into the sky.

Byrne switched on the radio and tuned in soft music. She went to Paula and said, "Will you dance with me?"

A new thrill rippled through the girl. She nodded and moved in close to Byrne.

She had often danced before but never like this. They hardly moved, yet Paula felt as if they weren't touching the ground. She fit into every curve of Byrne's body. They blended like two halves of the same person. The pressure of Byrne's palm on her back made Paula feel safe in surrendering. Dance became a prelude to love. Neither spoke as their bodies swayed in time to the music and developed a subtler rhythm of their own.

* * * * *

The newness of being together all night kept Paula from sleeping. She lay listening to the soft breathing of her beloved, wondering what dreams possessed her. Delicately, she kissed the arm flung across her. At last, because she was tired and because she was content, Paula joined Byrne in slumber.

She woke late the next morning. It took her a moment to realize that she was not in the lumpy bed at home. Her body felt different; not cramped and squeezed by the narrow mattress but relaxed and healthy. She felt a sudden impulse to leap up and run naked through the rooms but lay still so as not to waken Byrne. Sunshine fell in stripes of warm yellow on her beloved's skin. She watched the glistening russet color of Byrne's hair in the light. The relaxed face looked younger than it did when awake. The lines were smooth on her forehead, the little-girl freckles more apparent. Paula wondered what Byrne had been like as a child. She could not imagine she had looked different from the way she was at this moment.

Paula lay quietly for a long time, waiting for Byrne to waken. Full of the day's spirit, she grew impatient finally and leaned across to kiss her on the mouth, only lightly to stir her. Byrne turned her head and sniffed in sleep. Paula kissed her again and watched the eyelids flutter. Eyes still closed, a sleepy smile drifted across the face and lazily, Byrne returned Paula's kiss.

"You are here," she mumbled. "I was dreaming you had slept beside me."

"I did," Paula said.

"Yes." She drawled the single word as though it were the key to life's secrets and happiness.

Paula showered in the tile bathroom, letting the water spray steaming hot against her. She put her head under to feel her hair pushed forward by the force of the needles. Having found a bottle of shampoo on the shower floor, she squeezed cold liquid onto her scalp and rubbed vigorously, inhaling the soap's perfume.

Reluctantly, she stepped out of the stall, and called to Byrne for a towel. Byrne brought in two, threw one over Paula's head and began rubbing her back with the other.

"I think I used all the hot water," Paula said, surrendering herself to the pleasure of the energetic toweling against her skin.

Byrne chuckled without answering and Paula realized that you didn't use up all the water here because you couldn't. When will I learn? There's so much, she thought.

While Byrne was taking her own shower, Paula went out to buy a paper. She really wanted to stay at home, alone with Byrne, but she had said there were art exhibits they should see.

Together they went over the entertainment section while Byrne explained what the different galleries had to offer. She stopped in the middle of a sentence, suddenly, and smiled at Paula. "You're not listening, are you, darling?"

Paula had to admit that she wasn't. Sunday was for lounging at home and enjoying each other. A day for doing little things that people do together. Maybe taking a walk later on and inspecting shop windows.

"Every day," Byrne said, "you show me how to appreciate something I'd hardly noticed before. It would never occur to me to go for a quiet stroll on a

Sunday. The way you put it makes the idea seem marvelous. After a while one gets caught in the race to keep busy and do something, anything at all so that you needn't think. It's a terrible trap, and you make me realize it. You'll have to re-educate me, Paula. I need a few lessons."

Paula had no reply. Of all the things in the world, re-educating Byrne was hardly something she had thought possible. Byrne should be the teacher, if either of them had to be. Her confusion disappeared abruptly; she understood that learning was a mutual thing, that two people in love taught each other. Recognizing again that Byrne did love her, Paula felt a wave of gladness and gratitude rush through her.

Byrne dressed and put on comfortable shoes. Both of them bundled up against the cold. They might not be able to stay outside long, but a restaurant would always be at hand to warm them with coffee; besides, they would be together.

They strode briskly along the streets and Paula watched Byrne's cheeks whipped pink by the wind. She looked more vital and healthy, more beautiful, than Paula had ever seen her.

Later that afternoon they went to a movie and Byrne reached for Paula's hand beneath the protection of her folded coat. They had dinner in Chinatown and came home late that night, happy with each other and pleasantly tired.

Byrne said, "Maybe you should sketch."

Paula said, "Maybe you should sketch." They laughed and dawdled till Paula began to yawn but before they went to bed, there was something she wanted Byrne to tell her. She knew it was a childish question, yet she must have Byrne's opinion before she could make her own final decision on the matter.

They were sitting on the bed, half undressed, when Paula brought it up. "What we're doing," Paula began. "Is what we're doing wrong or are other people stupid?"

Byrne was hanging up her skirt. She finished pinning it and came over to Paula. Taking off the girl's shoes, she said, "I wish I could help you, darling. That's a question like which came first, the chicken or the egg."

"Well, what do you think? You must think something about it. After all, it's a whole way of life."

"I think it's right for some people and wrong for others."

"It's right for us, isn't it?"

Byrne set the shoes neatly beside each other and stood up. "It's right for me, anyway. And I can't stand here and tell you that you shouldn't love me. All I can say is that I'm doing my best to make you happy. I need you enough to turn handsprings if necessary. Let's not involve ourselves with the question of morals."

Paula was thinking about the man in the restaurant. She had realized, then, for the first time, that her love for Byrne made her different and set her apart. Yet everyone was entitled to be in love and no love could be more beautiful than Paula's love for Byrne. Yet she knew now that they must hide their feelings, sometimes, no matter how wonderful their love. Something in Paula screamed against that pain and injustice, but she did not forget that loving

Byrne was as natural and right for her as marriage and children were for others. The world did not matter; love did. Byrne mattered; and Byrne was Paula's world.

"I can make my own decisions," she finally said. "We can forget about it."

A long time after Byrne had fallen asleep that night, Paula lay awake in thought. How could it be wrong to do something that interfered with no one else? If they led a useful life together, what justice could there be in condemning them? She remembered how some of the fellows on her block made fun of the mincing, effeminate men who would sometimes pass them on the street. Neither she nor Byrne was trying to imitate the other sex. In a group of fifty women, could anyone pick them out as Lesbians? Paula rolled the unfamiliar word around on her tongue. Lesbian. That was something in short hair and trousers. Like Greta.

How horrible to look like Greta. How wonderful to look like Byrne. If she were tall and walked so gracefully and wore clothes the way Byrne did, she really would not care what people called her. Byrne was a woman. A real woman. A Lesbian too? Well, so what?

Then the recollection of Greta began to concern her. Undoubtedly, she would be coming back one of these days. Expecting to stay over, maybe. How would she react to Paula's presence? Would she understand? Would Byrne tell her that Paula was living here now? There must be no more ripped curtains, no more violence here in Paula's new home. She would not allow Greta to damage Byrne any more.

Perhaps she worried for nothing. Byrne knew

what she was doing when she asked Paula to live with her. She would trust Byrne and not question.

Paula awoke automatically at seven on Monday morning. No alarm called her. She opened her eyes knowing that she should dress and go to the office. The idea of returning to that work-a-day world felt pleasantly familiar. But to leave Byrne? Maybe it wouldn't be too terrible if she didn't go in. Certainly, she wasn't so important that they would miss her. Byrne lay fast asleep, and instead of slipping out of bed, Paula snuggled back under the covers. Her first responsibility was here, after all — to Byrne, who would miss her, who would spend a lonely day if she was gone.

She couldn't fall asleep again, and, after a while, went into the kitchen to start fixing breakfast. They would use the day well, she thought. Byrne would finish her portrait and she could concentrate on learning how to make an arm look three-dimensional. She had noticed the volumes on the bookshelf and was eager to study them.

About an hour later, Byrne strolled into the kitchen, the remains of a frown clinging to her forehead. "I woke up in that big bed and you weren't there."

Paula threw her arms around her neck. "Of course, I'm here," she said. "I decided not to go back to work so that we could be together."

"It's a good thing," Byrne replied.

They had breakfast and Paula insisted upon doing the dishes instead of leaving them in the sink for later. She couldn't understand how the place stayed so neat; Byrne never seemed to do anything to keep it clean.

Byrne shrugged. "I guess it jumps together by itself."

They should have a maid, Paula thought. That would be money well spent. But there were two things Byrne couldn't stand. One was having a maid. The other was driving her own car. "They both require supervision when you least feel like supervising," she said.

Learning about the small things that Byrne liked or didn't like was an adventure. She didn't care for sugar in her coffee at breakfast but she took three cubes at lunch time, Paula remembered.

Paula had donned comfortable jeans and was already sketching while Byrne wandered around the house, slowly waking up. This was the best Monday morning Paula had ever spent, and the most industrious. She wondered why privileged children, who didn't have to slave at jobs they hated, got into trouble. Byrne finally climbed into a pair of faded denims. She rolled the legs halfway up her calves and slid into the sandals she loved. She came over and looked at Paula's picture.

"The only hope for you," she said, "is to observe more closely what you draw. This hurrying is a waste of time in the long run. You don't hurry in bed," and she kissed the back of Paula's neck. "Why should you when you draw?"

Paula blushed and slowed the movement of her pencil. Long-restrained energy pushed against her and she wanted to fill all the books with pictures. "How can I help feeling like this? There's so much to learn," she protested. "So much to do and I'm already an adult.

172

"Don't worry about that," Byrne said. "Let Grandma Moses be your guide."

Dutifully, Paula slowed her pencil and tried to observe more closely the various objects that she drew. By noontime, she was being quite cautious and Byrne complimented her on the improvement.

Yet Byrne herself did not seem to want to begin. Occasionally Paula mentioned the unfinished portrait. Byrne only brushed it off.

Paula wasn't discouraged. She knew that a very rare mood had gotten Byrne started in the first place. She would have to wait and move carefully so that Byrne would not feel she was being trapped. Of all the presents Byrne could give to Paula, a finished portrait of herself would be the most precious. First, of course, it would prove to Byrne that she could still work. Secondly, it would mean that Greta's influence had been annihilated.

So Paula was patient. She didn't speak of the picture any more that day. Nor the next or the one after that. They spent the week together in perfect harmony and it seemed to Paula that Greta had never existed.

On the following Saturday, her dream was suddenly shattered.

11

Paula dried the last breakfast dish and stacked it on top of the others in the closet. She hummed a little tune, planning how they should spend the day. A week of hard study lay behind her and Byrne wanted to reward her with a small vacation.

In the living room, Byrne was leafing through a magazine that listed all the Broadway plays. They had decided to go to the theater tonight. Now it was simply a matter of choosing a play so that Byrne could phone an agent for tickets.

Drying her hands, Paula sauntered in and stood looking over Byrne's shoulder.

"Would you like a musical?" Byrne said. "This one here got rave notices."

"Anything with laughs. How about that one with the four stars beside it?"

"If it isn't sold out," Byrne replied. She had taken a piece of toast in with her and Paula leaned over to brush the crumbs from her lap.

They were thus occupied and chattering happily about their evening when a knocking at the door interrupted them. Paula's first thought was that it might be Phil again. She stood firmly planted behind Byrne, determined this time not to hide.

Byrne threw the magazine aside. Her mouth pursed in annoyance at the interruption as she went to answer the door. She opened it and Paula heard Greta's peculiar flute-like voice. "You only called me once this week. Why haven't you called me?"

Greta suddenly bursting into her dream world shook Paula. With hurt surprise, she tried to remember when Byrne had made the phone call. It could have been any number of times when Paula went out for cigarettes. Why had Byrne done this behind her back?

To hide her hurt and disillusionment Paula said, "Ask her in, Byrne. You needn't carry on your conversation in the hall."

Byrne stepped aside without protest. Taking Greta's arm, she brought her into the room.

That same lurking smile on the photograph was on her lips, and seemed to fill the room. An evil, sweet smell, almost of incense, seemed to rise about her as she stood docile in the center of things. She played the smile on Paula as though the girl was a statue. The fine hair, young and soft, fell on the wrinkled forehead in light wisps of platinum.

"Byrne?" Greta's voice fluttered like a silken ribbon. "It's very lonesome in that room by myself. I keep thinking that you'll come get me but the door never opens. Don't you love me, Byrne? You said you love me." She stood without removing her coat until Byrne took it off for her. Only the blonde hair and the china blue eyes seemed alive in a face that was shattered. Her small frame was hidden under rolls of fat and encompassed in oversize trousers. The tiny feet encased in clumsy oxfords looked too fragile to hold her up.

"Of course I love you," Byrne said instantly, and Paula's heart cringed.

They don't know I'm here, she thought. I mean nothing. Nothing! She went to Byrne and took Greta's coat from her. Byrne hardly nodded a thank you.

"Why don't you introduce me to your friend?" Paula had to say.

"Oh yes, excuse me." Byrne collected herself. She returned to Greta and guided her to a chair. "I want you to meet this nice girl," Byrne said to her. "She draws very lovely pictures, too."

"Pictures?" Greta said. "I'd like to see some pictures." The ancient face puffed into a smile of tiny pointed teeth, baby teeth showing horridly in the ancient face.

"Of course, she'll show you her pictures. Won't you, Paula?"

She doesn't have to treat her like an infant, Paula

thought. She's no more of a child than I am. "Of course," Paula agreed. She got one of her pads from the easel and tossed it onto Byrne's knees. Byrne didn't notice that Paula was irritated. Her one object was to soothe Greta. Paula might as well be in Timbuctoo for all the difference her presence made.

Byrne opened the pad and showed Greta page after page of sketches. Paula watched closely from where she stood beside the bookshelf. She saw understanding in Greta's round eyes for the first time, not the easy delight of a child. "They're very nice," Greta said. "You must teach her not to make this same mistake." With a slender finger, she pointed to some lines that Paula could not see. She couldn't care less what Greta's opinion was, but Byrne listened intently to every word.

Paula said, "Byrne tells me you did that painting on the wall. It's very beautiful. I would like to see some others, if you would ever care to show them to me."

"Byrne has all my paintings." The music of Greta's voice wound itself through the room. "She has my paintings and my music records and my old photographs. You must ask Byrne to show them to you. She has all the pieces of my life packed away somewhere." She touched Byrne's cheek, wonderingly, as though it were a rare object. "Why don't you show them to us? I would enjoy it, too."

"Yes, why don't you?" Paula said.

For the first time, a hint of embarrassment came to Byrne's cheeks. The spell of Greta's presence held her, yet she struggled to be matter of fact. She looked at Paula with eyes that asked forgiveness in this situation.

"I would enjoy seeing them," Paula urged. Sick with the knowledge that Byrne did not want to bring these things out into the open, Paula kept a smile solidly on her lips. She had never seen Byrne entranced, almost hypnotized like this. And by a nothing. A no one. A personality that nearly didn't exist. Her Byrne, sophisticated, debonair Byrne, was acting more like a child than Greta was.

"If you wish," Byrne agreed. She got up and went to the storage closet in the hallway.

There was so much Paula wanted to say to this creature sitting so innocently with puffy hands folded on fat legs. I know what you're doing. You've been pretty clever, too. Now it's my turn.

She wanted to say these things, but Greta was paying her no attention. She had leaned back in the chair and closed her eyes when Byrne left the room, as though life stopped until Byrne came back.

Byrne brought in half a dozen unframed canvasses and a heavy black leather album. She sat down on the couch. Greta got up and placed herself on the right, close to Byrne. Paula had no choice but to sit on the other side.

Paula said, "Let's go through the album first. I love old photographs." She could hardly keep the nastiness from her voice.

"Yes, the photographs," Greta said, her voice quivering with delight.

Byrne put the album on her knees and slowly opened the cover.

Fascinated, Paula viewed the yellowing snapshots. Byrne and Greta at the seashore, drops of water gleaming on their sunburned shoulders. Byrne and Greta on horseback. Byrne and Greta holding a string of fish. Their close years of togetherness, so obvious from this album, made Paula cringe in the knowledge of what a tiny portion of Byrne's life she herself could fill.

Byrne dusted the pictures off as she turned each new page. Paula saw laugh wrinkles crease around Byrne's eyes as she relived each photograph. And Paula knew then only too well that Greta had little need to fight to keep Byrne; the strength of years did it for her.

There was nothing Paula could say as Greta and Byrne recalled incidents to each other with each picture. She could only sit there, very small and very silent, hoping that Byrne would come back to her soon.

When she had turned the last page, Greta sighed and put her head on Byrne's shoulder. Without saying a word, she held Byrne in complete possession.

At last Paula was driven to remind Byrne that the agent was holding theater tickets for them.

Byrne nodded as though she recognized her duty to Paula and gently moved herself from beneath Greta's head. She brought the woman her coat and helped her into it.

Greta didn't object. She wore a faraway smile that touched her lined forehead with a light finger. "I'll go to sleep tonight and dream about those pictures," she said.

Byrne accompanied her to the door and saw her into a taxi. When she returned, Paula faced her. Outrage trembled in every muscle of her body.

"Don't," Byrne whispered before Paula could say a word. She fell limply to the couch and rested her closed eyes on the heels of her hands. "I know

179

everything you're going to say and I don't want to hear it."

Paula tried to calm herself. The right words, the words that would endear her to Byrne, would not come. Prisoner of jealousy, she wanted to say things that would stab back at Byrne. She needed to hurt in return for the hurt.

"You lied to me," Paula said, her voice low with growing anger. She threw the album off the couch and slid it under the table. "You asked me to live with you and then you called her behind my back."

"Oh, please," Byrne pleaded, "let me be."

The anguish in her voice made Paula instantly contrite and full of guilt for her anger. She went to the couch and took Byrne's hands away from her face.

"If you love me, Byrne," she said, kneeling and holding the woman's face between her palms, "if you love me, that's all that matters."

"I do love you," Byrne said intensely. "You know that."

"Then let's not talk about it any more. We'll dress and go out just the way we planned."

"You're wonderful," Byrne said and kissed her lingeringly on the lips.

They took showers and Paula donned one of her new suits. She made herself chatter about unimportant things to convince Byrne that Greta didn't really disturb her. She was young, she was shapely, her chin line was smooth and graceful. Surely Byrne must appreciate this. Greta couldn't be taken anyplace without being stared at like a sideshow. It was a crime for Byrne to pull herself down to Greta's level.

Paula didn't feel any of the confidence she displayed. She was glad when they found their seats in the orchestra and the lights dimmed so Byrne wouldn't see the worry in her eyes.

Paula, engrossed in her thoughts, paid little attention to the show. She applauded when everyone else did, but her fingers were clenched around the program booklet. I've got to get Byrne away, she thought. If we stay in New York, I haven't got a chance against Greta.

After the last act, they crossed through traffic to a small restaurant. Surrounding them were happy faces of young couples out on their Saturday night dates. Girls in cocktail dresses laughed at their boyfriends' jokes. Older people sat quietly and enjoyed being with each other.

Paula ordered a Scotch and soda. Byrne didn't try to stop her.

"You know," Paula said after the waiter had placed their drinks on the table, "I think we could use a vacation."

Byrne smiled a slow understanding smile. She took her own glass and finished most of the drink. In the smooth forehead Paula noticed a wrinkle she'd never seen before. It came vertically to her eyebrow and disappeared in the golden arch.

"Well," Paula persisted, realizing her motives were quite clear to Byrne. "There's no use going through the same thing week after week. I need you to myself and you should give me the chance to have that."

The waiter placed menus before them but neither woman had an appetite. Paula lay her menu on the table and waited for Byrne's response to her demand.

"If you think distance will make a difference, let

me warn you beforehand. I've tried it." She shook her head. "There are some things you just can't kill."

"Don't you want to kill it? Honestly, Byrne, don't you?"

"As long as you live, my dear, I'm afraid you won't ever be able to understand what this is about." She sounded as though she were sorry for Paula.

Paula raised her glass and drank to push away the sound of that tone, to drown it out with clinking ice cubes. No scenes here. Only calm discussion as if they were talking about a new hat.

"How much does it take to understand," Paula said with her most adult manner, "that three people can't —"

"Be married?" Byrne finished for her. "So we're back to that again. My poor darling, why can't you realize that this game doesn't have any rules?"

The waiter returned and hovered at Paula's elbow.

Byrne ordered prime rib and Paula said the same to be rid of him.

"Rules or not," Paula said, "let's go away for a while. Maybe it'll work this time, just for me." She put on a cheerful expression.

"Whatever you say. I can't stand you being unhappy."

They picked through the meal and ordered a few more drinks each. Paula drank them without caring about the taste. After the third, she didn't taste anything, anyway. A giddy sensation made her feel quite confident. Pieces fell magically into place. A giggle rose in her throat and tumbled from her lips. Of course everything would be fine. Byrne was alive and here and hers. No freaky thing could take Byrne away from her. They would sail on a slow boat to Florida and never come back. Her unspoken secret emerged in more giggles.

"You're annoyed?" Paula hiccoughed.

"Let's get you home," Byrne said evenly. She glanced at the check and put a bill under the saucer. "You're drunk."

Riding home in the cab, Paula couldn't stop giggling. She wished Byrne wouldn't look so cross. She wished Byrne would sit closer to her and not stare out the window like that.

Inside the house Paula kicked off her shoes. She stumbled around the apartment until Byrne cornered her, pulled off her things and steered her into bed.

She clamped her eyes shut to fight off the dizziness that whirled the pillow round and round.

The next thing Paula knew a headache wakened her with an insistent pounding behind her eyes. She squinted into the daylight and groaned with discomfort. She felt beside her for Byrne but found only warm sheets and blankets.

Tensely, she lay wondering what had happened. The sound of Byrne's sandals on the linoleum in the kitchen reassured her. She put the pillow over her head to block out the sunlight.

Byrne came in and sat down on the edge of the mattress. "Drink this," she said. "It might help."

"No . . . no . . . no," Paula groaned from beneath the pillow.

"Come on, sit up." Byrne pulled the pillow away.

"The first hangover is always the worst. You'll get used to them after awhile."

Through the misery of her throbbing head, Paula wondered why Byrne wasn't angry with her for drinking. Obediently she sat up and downed the tomato juice. "Will I ever get rid of this?" she moaned.

"Who knows?" Byrne laughed.

Through bleary eyes Paula examined Byrne for traces of displeasure.

"Why should I be angry with you?" Byrne volunteered. "You're old enough for this sort of thing." She tucked the covers around Paula's waist and set the empty glass on the night table. "Heaven knows I'm not saint enough to bawl you out but you'd better start pulling yourself together, old girl. Unless you've forgotten everything."

"Oh, I remember," Paula said, engulfed by the recollected sadness. "Can we start packing today?"

"Yes. But don't make it sound like we're leaving forever. There's nothing worse than an exiled New Yorker."

Paula thought it wiser not to argue. If they went for a week, she could somehow stretch it into two. From there maybe to three. For all she cared, they could spend the rest of their lives travelling around the world. Anything to be away from the threat that dogged the happiness that had become her life.

12

Paula let Byrne decide where they would go. If only Byrne might become enthusiastic over some spot but they all seemed the same to her.

"I've always wanted to go to Florida," Paula said. The idea of swimming in February was the most fantastic thing she could imagine. Paula never dreamed she might loll on the beach like the girls in the newspaper ads.

"If that's what you want, it's fine with me."

Paula could hardly contain her delight. Surely Byrne would respond to aromantic far away place and nobody could walk in on them in the middle of . . . anything.

Paula had no summer clothes except for an old pair of sneakers lying in the bottom of her closet back home. Firmly she pushed out the thought of Ma and Mike. She hadn't phoned them for more than three weeks. She wished she could become invisible and go over there for a few minutes to see how they were doing.

"We'll get you all the clothes you need down South," Byrne interrupted her thoughts. "We'll fatten them up on the expense of your new wardrobe."

Paula, from her position on the bed, watched Byrne pull out two small pieces of luggage. "They're not big enough," Paula suggested, "even without my clothes."

"Remember, darling, we're going for a couple of weeks only. We don't need to take the whole house."

"That's not even room enough for both our lipsticks," Paula joked.

Byrne let the remark slide. She snapped the lids open and contemplated each valise in turn. "It's been a long time since I've used these," she said, not to Paula, but to herself.

With difficulty, Paula got out of bed and went to wash her face. She could not afford to let a mere headache get in her way now. She must keep Byrne at this business of packing, and she knew they must hurry. If Greta returned before they left, she might not be able to get Byrne away at all.

Paula splashed her cheeks with cold water and slipped into a black jersey dress. She tied her loose hair back and thought how much older she looked that way. The old casual appearance had left her. She seemed business-like and well-groomed. The windswept Paula had become a sleek woman. Her movements, in imitation of Byrne, were more graceful. Conscious of her posture and the gestures of her hands, Paula realized that in many ways she had experienced a lifetime in less than two months.

With the same joking attitude, she helped Byrne sort out and pack the articles which they would both need most and she continued to talk about Florida as though Byrne were taking her on a honeymoon.

Byrne phoned for plane tickets only to discover that they would have to wait until Wednesday. It had not occurred to Paula that they would have difficulty getting hotel reservations. She had developed the habit of thinking that Byrne's money could buy whatever she wanted, whenever she wanted it.

"Don't let it worry you," Byrne said. "We'll make arrangements to hire a car at the airport. Some motel is bound to have a spot open for us."

Paula remembered that Byrne didn't like to drive, and she was grateful to see how much Byrne was going out of her way to please her.

Although they had these few days before leaving, Paula insisted that everything be packed and ready to go immediately. She was tense with the dread of Greta returning before they left. The days to Wednesday loomed.

She made Byrne take her to museums and to the movies. She did anything to keep them out of the house in case Greta should call. The hours became a race in which she must stay always a few leaps ahead of Greta.

Sometimes at night when she lay in Byrne's arms, Paula would suddenly tense, thinking she heard steps coming toward the door. She could no longer abandon herself to the delight of Byrne's kisses. Paula's nerves, always alert, prevented her from experiencing the enchantment she had once been able to find spontaneously.

When Wednesday finally arrived, she fairly dragged Byrne out of the house and hailed a cab before the door was locked.

Only when they were seated in the plane did Paula relax. She fastened her seat belt and felt lightness return to her heart as they rose slowly to meet the clouds.

Thrilled with her first experience of flying, she watched the sparks shooting out from behind the propellers and looked down to the dots and patches of land that spread like a checkerboard below. "I'm glad you thought to take a day flight," Paula said, examining the white mountains that hung just beyond the edges of the plane's wings.

"That's all I could get," Byrne said. "I would have asked for it anyway," she responded to Paula's reproachful look.

"You're sweet and good and I love you," Paula whispered.

The stewardess brought them containers of coffee and slim halves of sandwiches wrapped in cellophane.

Byrne gave hers to Paula. "I'm saving my appetite for Miami," she explained.

Paula tried to believe it but she knew that Byrne's anxiety about Greta had taken up now when hers had stopped. She was glad when Byrne put her chair back and closed her eyes. At least she wouldn't have to keep up the chatter that neither felt like making.

Staring out into the acres of blue, Paula wondered if there was distance enough in the whole universe to escape from Greta.

Four hours later, the sign lit up in the front of the plane notifying the passengers that they were about to land.

Gently she took Byrne's arm. "We're coming in," she said eagerly, and Byrne yawned.

They stepped out into the brilliant sunlight. Paula lifted her face to it and smiled.

"Look, Byrne, a palm tree!" Immediately she felt silly for behaving like a child.

"Don't stop yourself," Byrne said good-naturedly. The tropic sun made a flame of her hair and her eyes shone a clear emerald in the dustless air.

"How different it smells," Paula exclaimed as they walked to pick up their luggage. "I thought all cities had exhaust smoke around them."

"Wait till we get to the ocean," Byrne promised. "It'll knock you out if you go for clean smells."

Paula noted the lilt in Byrne's voice and thought: She's enjoying me now. I'm pleasing her again the way I did at first. I've got to remember not to nag her about anything. She realized, gleefully, that there was nothing here to nag Byrne about at all.

Byrne went to the office of a car rental agency and escorted Paula into a white Chevy convertible.

"Keep your eyes wide open, my darling. You're about to see the millionaires' playground." The flight had not tired Byrne and she didn't seem to mind driving.

189

They drove across the causeway and Paula gawked at the yachts anchored beside palace after palace. Spanish-style mansions — candy pink, gleaming white, baby blue — decorated the waterfront. The sight of all this sprawling wealth made Paula nearly weak. What could Byrne possible want with dirty crowded New York when they could live in spacious beauty like this?

"Byrne, can we afford this?" she said seriously. She'd never really considered Byrne's money before. It had meant nothing to her except that they didn't have to go to work every day.

Byrne laughed and pushed back a strand of hair that the breeze had blown into her ear. "Not quite all this. Did you want me to buy you Miami?"

"Oh, you know what I mean. Could we maybe have a little house?"

"Don't be so hasty. You might tire of it in a few days."

"Never. It's too magnificent." And she wondered if Byrne was tired of it already.

They pulled up to a breathtaking motel such as Paula thought existed only in the movies. She held herself very straight and followed Byrne into the lobby. Luckily, a family had just vacated a suite of three rooms and the manager was glad to show it to them. As if they wouldn't like it!

The bedroom overlooked the ocean. Paula stood at the wall-length window gazing speechless at the turquoise water banded far out by a ribbon of violet. Small crests of white rolled in toward the sandy shore. The beach stretched on either side, dotted here and there with people. Who could ever leave this for the mobs of Coney Island?

190

"This will be fine," Byrne said and went with the manager to sign in.

Alone in the apartment, alone with the gorgeous view, the warmth and relaxation spilling against her strained nerves, Paula felt tears rising in her eyes. She had no reason to cry. She felt so wildly happy, the mere idea of tears was ridiculous. Yet they streamed down her cheeks. Unable to bear the beauty of what she saw, she turned her back to the window. Her mind flitted without sense from object to object as her gaze wandered around the room.

Byrne came back, a bellhop behind her carrying the valises. Paula went into the kitchen until Byrne had tipped him and shut the door.

Then she ran out and flung her arms around Byrne, pressing her head hard against her breast.

"Why, what's the matter?" Byrne said, holding her away and frowning at the streaming tears.

"Nothing," Paula choked. "I can't bear all this happiness."

"Let's not make it a funeral," Byrne chided. "Stretch out for a while and take a nap. Remember, we have to get you a bathing suit and things."

"Will you lie down with me?"

"I can't sleep during the day. Especially not with that television going."

Paula laughed through the tears and turned the set off. "Now come lie down, too."

"No, really. It'll only make me restless. I'll stay here in this chair right beside you. Or better still, I'll bring us back a few snacks."

The idea of Byrne going out without her made Paula uneasy. She recalled the telephone and how easy it would be for Byrne to place a long distance call. "I'm all right," Paula insisted. "Wait a minute until I freshen up and we'll go out together." She felt like a jail keeper, but it had to be done.

They strolled a few blocks and found rows of stores displaying shorts and beach attire. She wanted only a few things. Byrne bought her a trunkful. Paula didn't protest, realizing that Byrne was trying to make up for the unhappiness of the past few days.

She pumped up her reserves of energy and let Byrne take her sightseeing. The way Byrne was cramming so much activity into the one day made her uneasy. They had endless time in which to do these things but Paula stopped herself from saying so aloud.

By eight o'clock, she was exhausted. They were strolling along Collins Avenue surrounded by the flash of sun-tanned women in blonde hair and loud jewelry, attracting the attention of men casually but just as flashily dressed.

Paula took Byrne's arm and stopped her in the middle of the street. "Take me home and put me to bed," she pleaded.

"Oh baby, I'm sorry," Byrne said. "I thought you were enjoying this."

"I am. But it's enough for one day."

"Okay. Let's find the car."

Byrne maneuvered through the traffic and they sped back toward the motel. The evening wind blowing from the ocean laid its brisk salt odor on Paula, lulling her closer and closer to sleep.

When they reached their rooms, she unbuttoned her things and left them on the floor where they fell. She crawled beneath the cool sheets and waited for Byrne while she took a shower.

Paula tried to stay awake. Away from Greta, alone with the woman she loved, she ached with desire — to hold her beloved and run her lips and hands over every inch of her body, to make love to her again with the freedom and joy that this one day had returned to her.

Paula lay on her back, spread out on the wide bed, feeling the night air roll over her body with its almost human caress. She listened to the shower splash on the tile and imagined Byrne standing, glistening with droplets of water sliding down her breasts. Glancing out the window, she saw palm trees silhouetted in the moonlight, and the waves of the ocean seemed painted with silver. She tasted salt on her lips and it was good. In contentment and fatigue, she sighed and closed her eyes.

Byrne, refreshed and sweet-smelling, crawled in beside Paula, who lay in heavy, relaxed and peaceful sleep.

The night slid by dreamlessly for Paula. She awoke next morning transfused with new life, her body elastic with energy. She leaped out of bed and ran to the window, a beaming smile on her face to greet the gorgeous expanse of sea and sky.

"I can't believe it," she trilled, standing nude at the window and stretching her arms wide, wanting to take the world into her embrace. "We're really here. It's not a dream after all."

Byrne, who had been up for awhile and was folding their things into drawers, said, "Hey, get away from there. Want to be arrested as an exhibitionist?"

Paula ducked quickly to the wall, blushing. "I can't help it," she exclaimed. "Everything is so — spectacular."

"Put this on and we'll go for a dip before breakfast." She tossed Paula the new bathing suit of black and white striped knit.

She wriggled into it and turned her back for Byrne to hook the straps.

"You're marvelous in this thing," Byrne murmured. "I'll have to fight for you on the beach."

Paula swung around and examined Byrne, starkly magnificent in her own black suit. Her firm, rounded breasts and long waistline blending into the lean hips made a breathtaking picture as Paula had seen only in magazines. That a live person could be carved so perfectly seemed incredible. "We'll have to fight for each other," Paula trembled.

Byrne patted her behind and affectionately pushed her out the door.

They flung themselves into the ocean and dived beneath the tepid waves. The crystal pure water and sparkling sunshine brought surging vitality to them both. They rubbed themselves briskly dry and went for breakfast.

Later that afternoon, Byrne took Paula water skiing. They sank together, and surfaced spluttering, laughing. At night, they took a midnight ride in the moonlight. Their silent glances met again and again in mute caress, filling them both with total love and desire. Alone in their rooms at last, the rising passion of romantic love blended with the glowing headiness of a tropical night. Their love-making was long and languorous, gentle and tender, and finally an all-encompassing ecstatic storm.

"I love you," Byrne said later. And Paula knew that it was so.

The days grew into a pattern of bliss which seemed to be awakening new youth in Byrne. Paula seldom caught her brooding now. Her skin became an Indian bronze and the spray of freckles spraying across her nose made her face, at times, like a little boy's.

In the darkness, when Paula held Byrne and listened to the rhythmic peaceful breathing, she thanked heaven for being so kind to her at last.

Then, as Paula was trying a new lipstick one day, smiling appreciatively at her own reflection, Byrne said the words she had almost forgotten existed.

Byrne took off her sunglasses and laid them on the dresser. "It's time," she said simply.

Paula halted with lipstick poised in mid-air like a rabbit fascinated by the gleaming eyes of the oncoming snake. She waited without answering for Byrne to continue.

"We can't go on like this forever."

Paula bit her lip as she lay down the lipstick, bolstering herself inwardly. "Yes it can go on," she said with desperate conviction. "You said we could afford a little place. Why don't we rent a small house or maybe an apartment if you'd rather? We can buy drawing equipment and work just as hard down here as anywhere."

Byrne came to her and took her hands. Her hair, bleached redder by the sun, curled lightly with the salt water of swimming. "My darling, don't be afraid. Please trust me and know that what I'm doing is right. Living here is only a way of avoiding the issue. We can't remain forever with something hanging over our heads. Do you want us to be running like escaped convicts for the rest of our lives? We must go back. Surely, you feel that I love you completely. Believe me, nothing threatens that love. Nothing."

"If that's true," Paula groped around for some argument, "then we can stay. We don't have to look for trouble deliberately." She pleaded silently for Byrne to agree.

The woman's eyes were steady and bright with smiling. "I don't blame you for fighting after all that has happened, but I wish that you could have faith in me, this once."

Paula didn't answer. With heavy heart, she pulled the valises down from the closet shelf and started to fold her clothes.

13

Their flight home felt to Paula like a cold, inevitable, almost ominous thing. The motors droned gloomily in her ears and she hid herself from Byrne behind the pages of a novel.

A taxi brought them to the familiar brownstone house. Paula stood in the musty apartment and stared out at the leafless trees now bent by a howling March wind.

Byrne tried to make conversation, tried to joke and chatter with Paula as they had in the Florida sun. Yet Paula held herself aloof, answering in monosyllables, if at all.

They went to sleep that night with the suitcases still untouched. Paula felt that the joy of Miami had been locked away from them forever. It was just a matter of time before Greta would come once more to spin her evil web, to confuse and clutter, perhaps demolish their happiness. She lay stiffly under the blankets, wanting to smash this place out of existence.

When Monday came, Paula was not surprised to see Byrne dress and put on her coat. She didn't ask where Byrne was going.

"Not even a little smile for me?" Byrne said, pulling on her gloves and mimicking Paula's pouting mouth. "Just a teensy-weensy smile for your adoring slave?"

"When I know where you're going, how can I smile?" she said bitterly.

"Ah, well," Byrne replied with undefeatable good nature. "Maybe when I come back, you'll change your mind." Her spirits seemed to be holding a secret difficult to keep to herself.

Paula ignored everything. She folded her arms across her chest and half turned away from Byrne and did not answer the "I'll be home soon" that Byrne tossed gaily into the room as she shut the door behind her.

For minutes Paula sulked, staring into space, cursing herself as a fool. How long was she going to put up with this? If her love meant anything to Byrne, they would never have come back. She would always be second fiddle to a freak!

The hours went by. In her anger Paula didn't

198

notice them pass. Eventually Byrne would return. She would come in and make love to Paula as if nothing had happened while she was gone, as if they were both completely free. Paula burned with resentment.

Lunch time came and went. The hunger pains in Paula's stomach went unheeded as she recalled the lovely dinners they had shared in the violet dusk. She paced around the room, opened a book, flung it down. Shadows of evening grew longer across the room. The street lamps came on but she stayed in the darkness, rebelling against time, Greta, the world. When nine o'clock passed, a slight tremor of fear tapped at her heart. Refusing to surrender, she flung herself on the couch and shouted angry words into the empty silence. By ten o'clock, she was peering out the window.

When the phone rang, Paula jumped.

Then she restrained herself and let it ring a few times.

Worry, she whispered to an imaginary Byrne. Worry a little about me for a change.

At the ninth ring she picked up the receiver and said, "Hello," with stiff casualness — as it clicked down at the other end.

"Byrne?" she said quickly. "Byrne?"

Too late.

She'll call again, soon, Paula told herself, forcing her fingers to let the receiver go so it could ring. She thinks I went for milk or something.

She glared at the phone. She'll call, she said again and made a fist and bit into the knuckles.

"Ring. Dammit. Ring."

Silence. She hovered over the receiver, commanding it, her breath lurching in angry gulps, then trembling in remorseful commotion. What did Byrne want? Why did she phone instead of coming home? She recalled Byrne's airy, "See you soon." It was eleven thirty now. Long past soon.

"Where are you?" she shouted into emptiness.

What did you need to tell me?

Maybe it was someone else. A wrong number. An obscene caller losing his nerve. No excuses soothed. She paced around and into the kitchen, then back again. Nothing to do but wait . . . glaring at the phone, threatening it, arguing, pleading and finally begging, "Please ring."

Fifteen minutes later, she heard steps at the door and ran to it, everything forgiven, ready to leap into Byrne's embrace.

She flung the door wide.

"Byr . . ."

The name died on her lips as she saw the upstairs neighbor smiling at her uncertainly with a folded piece of paper, hand poised in the act of slipping it into the door.

"Pardon me," he said. "You're Paula?" He introduced himself as Paula murmured yes. "Byrne phoned and left this message for you. She thought you weren't home."

Paula barely managed a civil, "Thank you," as she snatched the note, dashed inside and opened it, leaning heavily against the door, legs trembling, hands trembling.

A phone number. The rest of the paper blank.

She snatched up the phone and dialed.

After the twenty-fifth ring she hung up and dialed again.

No answer.

No answer.

No answer.

She gave up, her palms were wet and hot. Darkness seeped into the room, bringing thoughts of Greta and dread. She snapped lights on to destroy the shadows. Sickly premonitions turned her flesh clammy.

This was not Byrne's idea of retaliation. She wouldn't play hard to get. Byrne was above childish pettiness. If she didn't answer, there was good reason why not. Wherever Byrne was, something was wrong. Terribly, drastically wrong.

What to do . . . what to do . . .

Where did Greta live?

Telephone information didn't help. The operator insisted on protecting privacy paid for with an unlisted number.

Paula paced the rooms, patting her cheeks rapidly, her mind whining in high idle.

In the alcove where Byrne kept her business matters, she paused before Byrne's desk, glared at the metal box on it, then flipped the cover back and tore through Byrne's file of private papers, throwing things around, her heartbeat sensing that time, time, time, mattered and nothing else. At the back, bundled in a tired rubber band, she found old insurance forms filled out for Greta with an address.

Coatless, Paula ran out into the middle of the street. Cars squealed around her, drivers honked and cursed while she flailed both arms to stop a taxi.

Greta's name was not in any of the bell slots

above the brownstone stoop. Paula scanned up and down the smudged tabs a second time then pressed the button for Janitor.

An irritated woman hobbled up from a basement apartment, chewing something with garlic.

Paula apologized for disturbing her and asked which was Greta's apartment.

"Moved out two months already. Thank God."

"Where to?"

"I don't know. Only quiet tenants I know."

"I have to find her. Her sister is dying in a hospital in Kansas. Greta is her only living relative."

The woman paused on the step. Her jaw stopped and she studied Paula. "Dying? Yeah? What ailment?"

"An abortion."

Paula ran down and grabbed the woman's lumpy hands and clung to them and stared her earnestly in the eyes until she broke down into understanding and agreed that yes, this juicy gossip was a matter of life and death.

"Come. I have it in my register someplace. I'll look it up for you."

By the time Paula sprinted to the second floor, the major excitement was over. Neighbors still loitered in the hall, buzzing amongst themselves at a distance from an open door at the far end of the hallway glaringly lit.

Paula shouldered through, saying, "What happened? . . . Anybody hurt?"

Anybody killed? she was thinking but couldn't bring herself to ask.

"Guns should be outlawed."

"What people do to each other . . ."

"Maniacs."

"Lezzybeans."

She crept into the apartment and it was difficult to tell that murder had not been done.

Overturned chairs and clothing fragments shrieked horror, madness. Blood . . . yes, it must be blood . . . stained darkly a pale raffia mat dragged askew in what was left of the living room. The walls went black for one spinning moment. Paula clutched her rib cage, supporting her lungs against sticking pains with every breath. Easy enough to piece together the developments . . . how Byrne had come here . . . how she had tried and failed to calm Greta's black mood . . . how despair had escalated into violence until, finally, Byrne called her . . . to ask for something on that ringing phone . . . which would ring forever in Paula's ears, calling for the help she had been too arrogant, too self-centered to give. She backed from the apartment and tried to light a cigarette but could not connect the match flame with the tobacco.

Outside on the steps she asked a neighbor, "Where were they taken?"

"New York Hospital is the closest."

The emergency room entrance opened into chaos. People in bandages seeping blood, babies shrieking, prostrate bodies on gurneys in every corner.

Wounded-looking eyes, silent eyes stared at her, at walls, at nothing.

Paula flung herself against the admitting counter and asked and asked again.

"Was a Byrne Evans brought in earlier?"

The clerk shrugged blankly. She didn't recall or wasn't on duty at that hour and had no time now to oblige and look through records.

"Oh yes," a nurse said who overheard. "*Those* two." She sighed at Paula. "I'm not sure visitors are allowed."

Paula waited in front of a television set glaring down at her with imperial poise. Ten minutes later, an aide told her a room number and directions.

She stumbled through labyrinths, rode elevators, glanced bleary-eyed at wall signs and trotted and walked until she reached a door slightly ajar.

She had come what seemed like miles. Now she stood, unable to manage the next ten steps inside.

Then she was through the doorway and at the foot of Byrne's bed, straining to understand Byrne's bandaged head and white face and closed eyelids. Sleeping? Sedated? . . . Horrible choices snaked leadenly through Paula's mind.

"Can you tell me anything?" she murmured to a nurse in heavy green mascara who came in and went directly to feel along the clear plastic tube connected to a bottle hanging upside down and to a needle at the other end, taped to Byrne's left forearm inside near the elbow.

The nurse said, "She's doing fine," without looking at Paula. The words rattled dryly, encouraging as cereal dregs inside an empty cardboard box.

Paula brought a chair to the bedside and sat down and stared at Byrne and listened to her breathing. She felt her own fingertips rippling with cold. She shivered in small waves of nausea and forced them away.

"She's unconscious, isn't she?"

"Just sleeping, dear." The nurse felt underneath the cover and seemed satisfied with what she found. "She'll open her eyes soon, you'll see."

"Who is her doctor?"

"It's on the chart, dear. Let's look. Oh. Dr. Leamis. Ken Leamis. He's very good."

"Will he be coming in tonight?"

"Not until morning, most likely. I don't think he's doing rounds."

Nobody was talking, nobody saying anything definite, which meant to Paula there must be plenty to say.

She leaned over and murmured in Byrne's ear. "Live . . . live . . . live . . ." prepared to sit here and brainwash her through the night. She can't die because of my stupid arrogance. Calling me for help. Depending on me . . .

"Visiting hours are over," the nurse had, and removed a lipstick tube from a pocket.

The next morning brought no change in Byrne's condition.

A whole night had passed and still she lay behind thick silence. A different, older nurse read the chart and said a neurologist had examined Byrne hours ago. Visiting time and doctors' rounds did not coincide, apparently. I'll have to phone him, Paula thought.

Would he speak to her? Tell her the facts? What rights could she say she had concerning Byrne? What rights did she have?

She leaned to Byrne's ear and began again. "Live . . . live . . . live . . ."

A hand on her shoulder interrupted the stream. Paula saw the operating room shirt and baggy pants beside her. She looked up into a young face, blond haired with warm chestnut eyes, casual and friendly, for a surgeon.

"I'm Dr. Leamis," he said mildly. "We can have a word together after I examine our patient."

"Thank you," she said gratefully and aware then, that she was the only one who'd come. "I'll wait for you outside."

The corridor was no man's land, a place of suspended living. Her lightheadedness swirled and spooked the logical plod of minutes. NO SMOKING, a sign demanded, thick, red, alarming. It made Paula want all the nicotine in history to burn and fume in her lungs. Her legs felt wooden, no sensation in the knees. She stood across from the door and stared at the handle and rubbed her watch face with a thumb.

Dr. Leamis came out thankfully soon, smiling at her. Was it a smile she could trust? Or a putting her off smile, so she would not crumble here and have to be handled. The hospital was too busy, the staff too overloaded for visitors to become patients.

"One day at a time," Dr. Leamis counselled, close

206

to her, a shoulder touching the wall. "She responded this morning, in ways she didn't, yesterday. Your . . ." he paused quizzically.

". . . friend," said with a lilt of pride.

". . . is making significant progress. Her vital signs are stronger. That's encouraging. I believe she'll come through nicely if she fights. Which I think she will."

"Fights? Fights what?" Paula said urgently. "She can die?"

"Not that. We were concerned about brain damage. The bullet grazed certain areas. I doubt there'll be serious involvement, though the tests can't tell us everything. Much of Byrne's recovery will be up to herself."

"You're saying she can become a vegetable," Paula mouthed dully.

"It's premature to say anything."

"Was she ever conscious?"

He nodded. "She's conscious now."

"Could I . . Should I go in to her?"

"She would probably enjoy the company."

Paula wasn't so sure. Would the sight of her to Byrne's eyes help or drive home her terrible loss of trust. She crept into the room.

Byrne's breathing seemed lighter, her closed lids lighter, too, somehow. Paula sat down again and assumed Byrne could hear.

"I just spoke with your doctor," Paula began, determined that a cheerful tone was the only possible approach. "He says you're doing well. He's very pleased with your progress. Isn't that wonderful? In a few days you'll be your old self I bet. You'll probably want things to make the time pass. Tomorrow I'll bring those magazines you were reading and read to you . . ." She chatted on at an easy pace, talking at random and without concern, she hoped. *Fight, my darling. Please. Fight.* "I'll bring you flowers. That's what this room needs. White miniature carnations and a tea rose or two. We'll see what the florist has fresh." The early light slid a brilliant crispness into the room and showed up Byrne's flat paleness, the emptiness, the lassitude, the lack of . . . *what is it?* Paula pleaded silently. *Give me a word. I would die for you. You know it's true, no matter what. Oh dear God. I love her so much. Let her know it. Please let her know.*

Paula saw a movement in Byrne's fingertips, the tiniest motion, like a beckoning. She reached over and touched them. She felt Byrne struggle, then, with supreme effort, and saw it in a shifting of her shoulders and in her throat . . . Her lips opened. She sighed. Paula put her ear close to Byrne's face and heard a thick, labored effort and then . . .

"Greta."

Paula sat in the hospital cafeteria stirring sugar into her fourth cup of coffee. The nurses had sent her away. They had to attend to Byrne in privacy.

Byrne had said enough, though. She'd said what mattered, giving over the key to what would make her fight harder to get well.

Why was it surprising? Why did she feel stepped on? Mangled? Of course it would be Greta. Always Greta. That's what mattered to Byrne. Fruitless, perhaps dangerous to oppose the inevitable. She must do something, instead, to support it.

With the fifth cup of coffee Paula made a decision and swung out of the cafeteria at a stride.

Access to Greta would first require a few fibs to some attending nurses — which couldn't possibly matter compared with what was at stake.

"No. I'm sorry. The intensive care unit has strict rules. Five minutes every two hours. Relatives only."

"I'm her niece. There's no one else. You understand."

"Five minutes, then. At twelve o'clock."

"Thank you. Thank you very much."

This is what you must do, Paula repeated silently while she waited, grooming her emotions for the ordeal. Bring Greta and Byrne together — find a way! — that will last Byrne for the rest of her life. You were a fool to believe you could separate these two. They belong to each other. They are each other . . . and you must be their courier, their go-between, now. Yes you must. You can't fail Byrne again.

An eerie sense of purpose resounded and sustained the truth she'd recognized long ago but would not admit, then, when her love for Byrne obscured everything, even Byrne herself.

If only she had seen that Byrne could never be hers. Selfishness, blindness don't win. They are transient victors at best. Weak-sister Annies, after all.

Twelve o'clock. With brisk steps, she followed behind the nurse, steeling herself to face Greta.

"Five minutes," the nurse warned and left her.

Tubes and bottles and cylinders and a machine beside the bed writing curves with every breath exhaled, obscured the human being that had been Greta. Paula waited a few steps from the bed, watching these mechanics until the door closed.

"Greta," Paula said, aware that she was speaking to a void.

She looked keenly at the flaccid face, cream colored around the nostrils, blue tinges darkening the lips. The bullet she had aimed at her throat was doing the job but gradually. Death played with Greta, teasing her, holding her at bay as love had done.

Greta's eyelids sprang wide. The pupils held a rigid, unearthly shine as they stared at Paula.

"Byrne?" she said with surprising strength, a rally of illusion torn from the bandaged throat, trailing after life as life already moved off.

"Yes," Paula murmured. "I'm here."

"I don't love you anymore," Greta rasped. A wild triumph flashed across her sightless eyes. "Don't love you . . ."

The voice and thought stopped, suspended in the middle of a breath.

Paula glanced sharply at the machine. The graph curve flattened and ran along in a single steady line. The hand outside the cover fell slightly.

She's gone, Paula thought, staring numbly, searching over the body, hearing its irrevocable silence.

Paula sat down beside it, unaware that she was sitting, humbled, angry, at a loss, gazing at the lifeless hand, the garnet ring, its bloodstone winking in the fluorescent glare.

Greta was dead — and Byrne lived.

Now what? Now what? Her mind, pounding against Greta's desertion and her own despair, suddenly thrust horror aside, separated from every feeling except a luminous need to exonerate Byrne from all possible guilt.

Quickly she worked the ring down the finger and off into her palm, her fist closing tightly, secretively around her prize.

The door to Byrne's room was shut. A sign hung there.

NO VISITORS.

She raced to the nurses' station in the center of the corridor. A nurse behind the window turned over pages of a medications log. Paula rapped on the glass for her attention. The woman looked up, recognized Paula and motioned her inside.

"Dr. Leamis ordered a unit of blood. She's having a transfusion now."

"Will I be able to see her later today?"

"That will depend on how she responds. The doctor will let us know when."

"I understand."

Yes, yes, she understood. Her good sense fought off depression and told her blood will make Byrne strong. She's not Greta's twin, after all. She's not going to die. An imp inside Paula laughed with derision. It whispered Byrne and Greta thrive on blood.

"I'm exhausted," Paula said aloud, which made no difference, it seemed, to anyone.

"How is she?" she said to Dr. Leamis at seven o'clock that night.

"She's wide awake."

"Blood made all the difference."

"The question is, can she sustain her strength."

"Oh yes she can," Paula told him, outrageous with her own necessity.

The doctor nodded his approval. "Wait until tomorrow to tell her so."

"Yes, all right," Paula agreed with difficulty.

She rode home to the apartment, set the ring on the mantle and stared at the stone.

"Speak to me ring. Speak," she demanded, hypnotizing herself, blending the story she would tell Byrne, when Byrne could listen.

A fresh, high, artificial color bloomed in Byrne's taut cheeks which Paula saw immediately as she came into the room the next morning. Byrne's eyes were open. They gleamed faintly, secretly apathetic, denying the rally that hemoglobin had left in a rush.

Paula carried a magazine. In case Byrne had heard her yesterday, she wanted a continuity of talk. She also carried a dozen carnations and brought them to Byrne's nostrils, then whiffed them herself.

"Your favorites," Paula said confidently. I'll surround you with everything you love and you'll have to get well. You won't be able to resist it.

"Greta?"

Paula caught her upper lip between her teeth. She could not give Byrne the news straight out, and the name still slapped her in the face but what could that matter.

She closed Byrne's palm around the ring. "I went to Greta yesterday," she began.

Byrne's eyes came alive.

"Saw her?"

"Yes. I saw her before . . . she . . ."

Byrne's fingers opened. She looked at the ring. Her eyelids fluttered. They closed. Something glistened between the lashes. Paula turned her face away.

"Greta hasn't left you," Paula began softly in stroking tones. "I went to her room and stayed with her awhile. She thought I was you. She believed you were sitting with her before she died. You were, you know, in your spirit. You can't imagine the contentment that brought her. You gave her peace, Byrne. She didn't die alone, she went contentedly, blissfully talking of you and other, better times." Paula's voice was strong, eloquent with her mission, her passion for Byrne to live well, no matter what, no matter without her. She went on, transforming Greta's final, darkened confusion into an elixir of shining love, a gift to Byrne of memories. "She talked as much as she could about your days together. That's what she remembered. How she loved you. How you loved each other. She took that with her. Her last words, her last experience was with you, and thinking I was you, she gave me that ring."

Paula moved slightly, just enough to observe Byrne turning the ring over and over in her fingers, gazing at it with thoughts that Paula could never

213

guess at. No hint in Byrne's features marred or illuminated the calm, the rising vitality. Yes that was it, vitality.

Next morning, Dr. Leamis confirmed that Byrne had begun to respond, her vital signs stronger, lifting her into the zone of independence.

This will last, Paula thought. That ring is the transfusion she needed. I have somehow absolved my darling. The horrors are washed away and she will live.

14

Paula went home to order her life, collect her clothes, pack whatever she would take. Apartment hunting would come next and then the search for a job. That was the order. She sat on Byrne's couch and gazed at the empty easel. So much to do by herself, for herself and alone.

At the end, in giving up, in giving these two women to each other, she sensed a balance, a relief in the rightness of her mind. Love, at least, still held its head high. Greta's unfortunate love. Byrne's. Her own. In the end, everyone wins or no one. She poured an inch of brandy into a glass and sipped it warm.

Her determination remained high while her energy divided between projecting plans that forced her into a future unimaginable without Byrne, and spending entire days at the hospital, forgetting her own life. In a stray newspaper in the smoking room, she found a squib about the shooting. How tiny it looked, how uneventful, how unimportant in the world. She read avidly of brawling and guns. The police had breezed through a routine investigation and concluded the obvious, the degrading. The write-up gave no details about the women, the personal lives and their meaning. Paula folded the paper and put it aside. The meaning was here, in this hospital. Byrne had known Greta would not go quietly to a sanitarium. When she'd said, "See you soon," Byrne must have had a premonition of violence and gone anyway, to risk whatever would happen, for Paula's sake. *And I wouldn't even smile for her when she left.*

She lay her head back against the upholstered chair and felt a warm streak of sunlight across her face and cried wearily, far back in her mind, where no one could see or hear.

Each day for three weeks, she watched Byrne growing stronger but she did not wear the ring, the precious messenger. Wrapped in a bit of tissue, it lay in the drawer where a nurse must have put it for her. Paula glimpsed it tucked away behind her brush and comb, almost hidden and did not pretend to understand Byrne's feeling.

On the twenty-seventh morning, Byrne began to talk a bit, slurring syllables during the first hours she tried. Paula smiled with that accomplishment, as though she were hearing the Gettysburg Address.

She had decided to stay with Byrne until Byrne went home. No need to discuss arrangements. By then both of them would be strong enough to resume their lives — separately.

Paula came in one morning and found Byrne sitting up with a tray before her of cups. The tube had been removed. Only a band-aid was left, covering the black and blue bruise.

"Mm good," Paula sang, inspecting the colorless liquids of food.

"I'm feeling free." Byrne smiled.

"Are you feeling hungry?"

Byrne shot her the old look of mockery. "Want some?"

A nurse said, "Your friend can have a cup of coffee if she'd like."

Paula quickly nodded yes. When it arrived, she lifted her cup. "Cheers to breakfast."

"Cheers to going home," Byrne said.

Paula blinked at her, startled, and felt the world begin to stir with challenges and pain and loneliness coming bleakly to life. The hospital routine had offered limbo which Paula accepted, protecting her from the future. Now that future was here, in Byrne's expectant concentration.

"Dr. Leamis gave me permission to leave on Friday."

"That's only three days away."

"Aren't you pleased?"

Paula realized her face must be split with conflict. "Of course I am," she said hurriedly. "It's wonderful news."

That night she moved her suitcases through the living room and stacked them near the door like little champions poised, ready to run. Run where? A hotel room. Any place. She considered leaving now, the wrench would be fast. Going now would save her from recriminations, from reliving what could not be undone and the futility of struggle, trying to rebuild a trust destroyed. Yet she could not walk out behind Byrne's back and surprise her nastily when she came home her first day. She remembered the first time Byrne had posed for her nude and smiled at the memory of her own nervous sketches. She had reached for the stars, for Byrne, and found hell. Easiest wasn't always best.

Friday morning, Paula strode through the hospital doors, fingers bunched into fists, her strength of resolve fainting before these last few hours with Byrne.

In the room, Byrne, already dressed, combed, and unsteadily seated, waited for the wheelchair that would take her to the street.

"Ready?" Paula said, a smile booming.

"Ready."

Paula wavered as Byrne stepped strongly into the

chair. She would ride home with Byrne, settle her and leave without a fuss. Perhaps next week they would talk about it, or next month, or a year from now, when they had settled into their different lives.

They started down the hall.

In the elevator Byrne reached a large envelope to her. "Look inside," she said quietly.

Paula stared at the hospital return address. There were papers inside it that weren't medical reports or prescriptions, she could tell, feeling the shape. What were they? Things that Byrne wanted out of the way? Things she hadn't the energy or interest to discuss? The cold, dooming business of business.

"Now?" Paula said, stalling.

"Now."

In the lobby, she opened the flap. The contents were instantly visible.

"Plane tickets?" she said, fingering two. "For today? To Florida?"

"Let's not go home," Byrne said as they entered the cab. "Let's go away for awhile. I need sun. You do, too. Look at that fading tan."

"Go away?" Paula said meekly. "Together?"

Byrne flung her a look of dark amusement. "Why would we take separate flights?"

Paula gazed dizzily into the hectic traffic thickening on the expressway to the airport. Her ability to reason shut down. One step at a time. Explanations would come. Or mercifully not.

On the plane, Paula covered Byrne's lap with a blanket. Byrne squeezed her hand beneath it and Paula felt for the ring beneath the glove.

"You'll never find it there," Byrne said calmly. "Greta despised that ring. She wore it in memory of her mother. How could you have known? You made up a beautiful story, my darling. I admired every word. I admired you. For the first time and at the worst time, you didn't despise Greta. You respected her, what she gave me and what we had together. You grew up."

Paula flushed. She looked away, into strata of clouds floating below the wing, hoping Byrne would not see the heat pulsing embarrassment and shame through her cheeks . . . and something new.

"I need you to have everything you want in the world," Paula said simply. "That's why I did it. You have to have everything you love."

She felt Byrne's finger touch her chin and turn her face and gaze directly into her, soaring through her soul . . . and gently say,

"Haven't I?"

A few of the publications of
THE NAIAD PRESS, INC.
P.O. Box 10543 ● Tallahassee, Florida 32302
Phone (904) 539-5965
Mail orders welcome. Please include 15% postage.

CHRIS by Randy Salem. 224 pp. Golden oldie. Handsome Chris
and her adventures.   ISBN 0-941483-42-8 $8.95

THREE WOMEN by Sally Singer. 232 pp. Golden oldie. A
triangle among wealthy sophisticates.   ISBN 0-941483-43-6   8.95

RICE AND BEANS by Valeria Taylor. 232 pp. Love and
romance on poverty row.   ISBN 0-941483-41-X   8.95

PLEASURES by Robbi Sommers. 204 pp. Unprecedented
eroticism.   ISBN 0-941483-49-5   8.95

EDGEWISE by Camarin Grae. 372 pp. Spellbinding
adventure.   ISBN 0-941483-19-3   9.95

FATAL REUNION by Claire McNab. 216 pp. 2nd Det. Inspec.
Carol Ashton mystery.   ISBN 0-941483-40-1   8.95

KEEP TO ME STRANGER by Sarah Aldridge. 372 pp. Romance
set in a department store dynasty.   ISBN 0-941483-38-X   9.95

HEARTSCAPE by Sue Gambill. 204 pp. American lesbian in
Portugal.   ISBN 0-941483-33-9   8.95

IN THE BLOOD by Lauren Wright Douglas. 252 pp. Lesbian
science fiction adventure fantasy   ISBN 0-941483-22-3   8.95

THE BEE'S KISS by Shirley Verel. 216 pp. Delicate, delicious
romance.   ISBN 0-941483-36-3   8.95

RAGING MOTHER MOUNTAIN by Pat Emmerson. 264 pp.
Furosa Firechild's adventures in Wonderland. ISBN 0-941483-35-5   8.95

IN EVERY PORT by Karin Kallmaker. 228 pp. Jessica's sexy,
adventuresome travels.   ISBN 0-941483-37-7   8.95

OF LOVE AND GLORY by Evelyn Kennedy. 192 pp. Exciting
WWII romance.   ISBN 0-941483-32-0   8.95

CLICKING STONES by Nancy Tyler Glenn. 288 pp. Love
transcending time.   ISBN 0-941483-31-2   8.95

SURVIVING SISTERS by Gail Pass. 252 pp. Powerful love
story.   ISBN 0-941483-16-9   8.95

SOUTH OF THE LINE by Catherine Ennis. 216 pp. Civil War
adventure.   ISBN 0-941483-29-0   8.95

WOMAN PLUS WOMAN by Dolores Klaich. 300 pp. Supurb
Lesbian overview.   ISBN 0-941483-28-2   9.95

SLOW DANCING AT MISS POLLY'S by Sheila Ortiz Taylor.
96 pp. Lesbian Poetry   ISBN 0-941483-30-4   7.95

DREAMS AND SWORDS by Katherine V. Forrest. 192 pp.
Romantic, erotic, imaginative stories. ISBN 0-941483-03-7   8.95

MEMORY BOARD by Jane Rule. 336 pp. Memorable novel
about an aging Lesbian couple. ISBN 0-941483-02-9   8.95

THE ALWAYS ANONYMOUS BEAST by Lauren Wright
Douglas. 224 pp. A Caitlin Reese mystery. First in a series.
ISBN 0-941483-04-5   8.95

SEARCHING FOR SPRING by Patricia A. Murphy. 224 pp.
Novel about the recovery of love. ISBN 0-941483-00-2   8.95

DUSTY'S QUEEN OF HEARTS DINER by Lee Lynch. 240 pp.
Romantic blue-collar novel. ISBN 0-941483-01-0   8.95

PARENTS MATTER by Ann Muller. 240 pp. Parents'
relationships with Lesbian daughters and gay sons.
ISBN 0-930044-91-6   9.95

THE PEARLS by Shelley Smith. 176 pp. Passion and fun in
the Caribbean sun. ISBN 0-930044-93-2   7.95

MAGDALENA by Sarah Aldridge. 352 pp. Epic Lesbian novel
set on three continents. ISBN 0-930044-99-1   8.95

THE BLACK AND WHITE OF IT by Ann Allen Shockley.
144 pp. Short stories. ISBN 0-930044-96-7   7.95

SAY JESUS AND COME TO ME by Ann Allen Shockley. 288
pp. Contemporary romance. ISBN 0-930044-98-3   8.95

LOVING HER by Ann Allen Shockley. 192 pp. Romantic love
story. ISBN 0-930044-97-5   7.95

MURDER AT THE NIGHTWOOD BAR by Katherine V.
Forrest. 240 pp. A Kate Delafield mystery. Second in a series.
ISBN 0-930044-92-4   8.95

ZOE'S BOOK by Gail Pass. 224 pp. Passionate, obsessive love
story. ISBN 0-930044-95-9   7.95

WINGED DANCER by Camarin Grae. 228 pp. Erotic Lesbian
adventure story. ISBN 0-930044-88-6   8.95

PAZ by Camarin Grae. 336 pp. Romantic Lesbian adventurer
with the power to change the world. ISBN 0-930044-89-4   8.95

SOUL SNATCHER by Camarin Grae. 224 pp. A puzzle, an
adventure, a mystery — Lesbian romance. ISBN 0-930044-90-8   8.95

THE LOVE OF GOOD WOMEN by Isabel Miller. 224 pp.
Long-awaited new novel by the author of the beloved *Patience
and Sarah*. ISBN 0-930044-81-9   8.95

THE HOUSE AT PELHAM FALLS by Brenda Weathers. 240
pp. Suspenseful Lesbian ghost story. ISBN 0-930044-79-7   7.95

HOME IN YOUR HANDS by Lee Lynch. 240 pp. More stories
from the author of *Old Dyke Tales*. ISBN 0-930044-80-0   7.95

EACH HAND A MAP by Anita Skeen. 112 pp. Real-life poems
that touch us all.   ISBN 0-930044-82-7   6.95

SURPLUS by Sylvia Stevenson. 342 pp. A classic early Lesbian
novel.   ISBN 0-930044-78-9   7.95

PEMBROKE PARK by Michelle Martin. 256 pp. Derring-do
and daring romance in Regency England.   ISBN 0-930044-77-0   7.95

THE LONG TRAIL by Penny Hayes. 248 pp. Vivid adventures
of two women in love in the old west.   ISBN 0-930044-76-2   8.95

HORIZON OF THE HEART by Shelley Smith. 192 pp. Hot
romance in summertime New England.   ISBN 0-930044-75-4   7.95

AN EMERGENCE OF GREEN by Katherine V. Forrest. 288
pp. Powerful novel of sexual discovery.   ISBN 0-930044-69-X   8.95

THE LESBIAN PERIODICALS INDEX edited by Claire
Potter. 432 pp. Author & subject index.   ISBN 0-930044-74-6   29.95

DESERT OF THE HEART by Jane Rule. 224 pp. A classic;
basis for the movie *Desert Hearts*.   ISBN 0-930044-73-8   7.95

SPRING FORWARD/FALL BACK by Sheila Ortiz Taylor.
288 pp. Literary novel of timeless love.   ISBN 0-930044-70-3   7.95

FOR KEEPS by Elisabeth Nonas. 144 pp. Contemporary novel
about losing and finding love.   ISBN 0-930044-71-1   7.95

TORCHLIGHT TO VALHALLA by Gale Wilhelm. 128 pp.
Classic novel by a great Lesbian writer.   ISBN 0-930044-68-1   7.95

LESBIAN NUNS: BREAKING SILENCE edited by Rosemary
Curb and Nancy Manahan. 432 pp. Unprecedented autobiographies
of religious life.   ISBN 0-930044-62-2   9.95

THE SWASHBUCKLER by Lee Lynch. 288 pp. Colorful novel
set in Greenwich Village in the sixties.   ISBN 0-930044-66-5   8.95

MISFORTUNE'S FRIEND by Sarah Aldridge. 320 pp. Historical Lesbian novel set on two continents.   ISBN 0-930044-67-3   7.95

A STUDIO OF ONE'S OWN by Ann Stokes. Edited by
Dolores Klaich. 128 pp. Autobiography.   ISBN 0-930044-64-9   7.95

SEX VARIANT WOMEN IN LITERATURE by Jeannette
Howard Foster. 448 pp. Literary history.   ISBN 0-930044-65-7   8.95

A HOT-EYED MODERATE by Jane Rule. 252 pp. Hard-hitting
essays on gay life; writing; art.   ISBN 0-930044-57-6   7.95

INLAND PASSAGE AND OTHER STORIES by Jane Rule.
288 pp. Wide-ranging new collection.   ISBN 0-930044-56-8   7.95

WE TOO ARE DRIFTING by Gale Wilhelm. 128 pp. Timeless
Lesbian novel, a masterpiece.   ISBN 0-930044-61-4   6.95

AMATEUR CITY by Katherine V. Forrest. 224 pp. A Kate
Delafield mystery. First in a series.   ISBN 0-930044-55-X   7.95

THE SOPHIE HOROWITZ STORY by Sarah Schulman. 176 pp. Engaging novel of madcap intrigue.   ISBN 0-930044-54-1   7.95

THE BURNTON WIDOWS by Vickie P. McConnell. 272 pp. A Nyla Wade mystery, second in the series.   ISBN 0-930044-52-5   7.95

OLD DYKE TALES by Lee Lynch. 224 pp. Extraordinary stories of our diverse Lesbian lives.   ISBN 0-930044-51-7   8.95

DAUGHTERS OF A CORAL DAWN by Katherine V. Forrest. 240 pp. Novel set in a Lesbian new world.   ISBN 0-930044-50-9   7.95

THE PRICE OF SALT by Claire Morgan. 288 pp. A milestone novel, a beloved classic.   ISBN 0-930044-49-5   8.95

AGAINST THE SEASON by Jane Rule. 224 pp. Luminous, complex novel of interrelationships.   ISBN 0-930044-48-7   8.95

LOVERS IN THE PRESENT AFTERNOON by Kathleen Fleming. 288 pp. A novel about recovery and growth.   ISBN 0-930044-46-0   8.95

TOOTHPICK HOUSE by Lee Lynch. 264 pp. Love between two Lesbians of different classes.   ISBN 0-930044-45-2   7.95

MADAME AURORA by Sarah Aldridge. 256 pp. Historical novel featuring a charismatic "seer."   ISBN 0-930044-44-4   7.95

CURIOUS WINE by Katherine V. Forrest. 176 pp. Passionate Lesbian love story, a best-seller.   ISBN 0-930044-43-6   8.95

BLACK LESBIAN IN WHITE AMERICA by Anita Cornwell. 141 pp. Stories, essays, autobiography.   ISBN 0-930044-41-X   7.50

CONTRACT WITH THE WORLD by Jane Rule. 340 pp. Powerful, panoramic novel of gay life.   ISBN 0-930044-28-2   7.95

MRS. PORTER'S LETTER by Vicki P. McConnell. 224 pp. The first Nyla Wade mystery.   ISBN 0-930044-29-0   7.95

TO THE CLEVELAND STATION by Carol Anne Douglas. 192 pp. Interracial Lesbian love story.   ISBN 0-930044-27-4   6.95

THE NESTING PLACE by Sarah Aldridge. 224 pp. A three-woman triangle—love conquers all!   ISBN 0-930044-26-6   7.95

THIS IS NOT FOR YOU by Jane Rule. 284 pp. A letter to a beloved is also an intricate novel.   ISBN 0-930044-25-8   8.95

FAULTLINE by Sheila Ortiz Taylor. 140 pp. Warm, funny, literate story of a startling family.   ISBN 0-930044-24-X   6.95

THE LESBIAN IN LITERATURE by Barbara Grier. 3d ed. Foreword by Maida Tilchen. 240 pp. Comprehensive bibliography. Literary ratings; rare photos.   ISBN 0-930044-23-1   7.95

ANNA'S COUNTRY by Elizabeth Lang. 208 pp. A woman finds her Lesbian identity.   ISBN 0-930044-19-3   6.95

PRISM by Valerie Taylor. 158 pp. A love affair between two women in their sixties.   ISBN 0-930044-18-5   6.95

BLACK LESBIANS: AN ANNOTATED BIBLIOGRAPHY
compiled by J. R. Roberts. Foreword by Barbara Smith. 112 pp.
Award-winning bibliography.   ISBN 0-930044-21-5   5.95

THE MARQUISE AND THE NOVICE by Victoria Ramstetter.
108 pp. A Lesbian Gothic novel.   ISBN 0-930044-16-9   6.95

OUTLANDER by Jane Rule. 207 pp. Short stories and essays
by one of our finest writers.   ISBN 0-930044-17-7   8.95

ALL TRUE LOVERS by Sarah Aldridge. 292 pp. Romantic
novel set in the 1930s and 1940s.   ISBN 0-930044-10-X   7.95

A WOMAN APPEARED TO ME by Renee Vivien. 65 pp. A
classic; translated by Jeannette H. Foster. ISBN 0-930044-06-1   5.00

CYTHEREA'S BREATH by Sarah Aldridge. 240 pp. Romantic
novel about women's entrance into medicine.
                                 ISBN 0-930044-02-9   6.95

TOTTIE by Sarah Aldridge. 181 pp. Lesbian romance in the
turmoil of the sixties.   ISBN 0-930044-01-0   6.95

THE LATECOMER by Sarah Aldridge. 107 pp. A delicate love
story.   ISBN 0-930044-00-2   6.95

ODD GIRL OUT by Ann Bannon.   ISBN 0-930044-83-5   5.95

I AM A WOMAN by Ann Bannon.   ISBN 0-930044-84-3   5.95

WOMEN IN THE SHADOWS by Ann Bannon.
                                   ISBN 0-930044-85-1   5.95

JOURNEY TO A WOMAN by Ann Bannon.
                                   ISBN 0-930044-86-X   5.95

BEEBO BRINKER by Ann Bannon.   ISBN 0-930044-87-8   5.95
      Legendary novels written in the fifties and sixties,
        set in the gay mecca of Greenwich Village.

VOLUTE BOOKS

JOURNEY TO FULFILLMENT	Early classics by Valerie	3.95
A WORLD WITHOUT MEN	Taylor: The Erika Frohmann	3.95
RETURN TO LESBOS	series.	3.95

These are just a few of the many Naiad Press titles — we are the oldest and
largest lesbian/feminist publishing company in the world. Please request a
complete catalog. We offer personal service; we encourage and welcome
direct mail orders from individuals who have limited access to bookstores
carrying our publications.